PUFFIN BOOKS

McBroom's Wonderful One-Acre Farm
and Here Comes McBroom!

Josh McBroom would rather 'sit on a porcupine than tell a fib', and when you read the tall tales in this book, that's a good thing to remember, for there are a lot of folk who just don't believe the stories he tells!

For instance, there's the time he bought an eighty-acre farm from Heck Jones for just ten dollars – a marvellous bargain, until he discovered that the eighty acres were piled on top of each other like a pack of cards, and were under water too. But then came the hottest day on record, when the sun came out and dried up the water, leaving the McBrooms with one acre of 'topsoil so rich it ought to be kept in the bank!' In fact, they found they could plant and harvest three crops a day!

Then there was the time when McBroom grew the biggest ear of corn ever seen, and the unforgettable occasion when the McBroom children planted Mexican jumping beans; and the time of the big wind; and the occasion when the whirlwind swept the topsoil clean away, leaving a one-acre hole in the ground . . .

But still, the McBrooms are able to keep their one-acre farm going despite the problems nature puts in their way, and the desperate attempts of greedy Heck Jones to cheat them out of their fabulous acre!

Sid Fleischman's collection of stories has a wonderfully funny, earthy folktale quality, and Quentin Blake's illustrations add his own touch of genius.

Sid Fleischman won the Mark Twain Award in 1977.

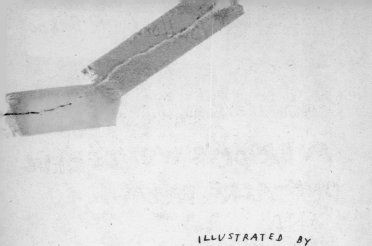

ILLUSTRATED BY
QUENTIN BLAKE

SID FLEISCHMAN

McBROOM'S WONDERFUL ONE-ACRE FARM AND HERE COMES McBROOM!

Puffin Books

Puffin Books, Penguin Books Ltd, Harmondsworth, Middlesex, England
Viking Penguin Inc., 40 West 23rd Street, New York, New York, 10010, U.S.A.
Penguin Books Australia Ltd, Ringwood, Victoria, Australia
Penguin Books Canada Ltd, 2801 John Street, Markham, Ontario, Canada L3R 1B4
Penguin Books (N.Z.) Ltd, 182–190 Wairau Road, Auckland 10, New Zealand

First published separately in the U.S.A. by W. W. Norton & Company, Inc.
McBroom's Wonderful One-Acre Farm first published in Great Britain
by Chatto & Windus Ltd 1972
Here Comes McBroom! first published in Great Britain
by Chatto & Windus Ltd 1976
Published in one volume in Puffin Books 1979
Reprinted 1985

Made and printed in Great Britain by
Richard Clay (The Chaucer Press) Ltd, Bungay, Suffolk
Set in Monophoto Ehrhardt

M^cBROOM's
WONDERFUL
ONE-ACRE
FARM

McBROOM'S
WONDERFUL
ONE-ACRE
FARM

CONTENTS

MCBROOM
TELLS
THE
TRUTH

THERE has been so much tomfool nonsense told about McBroom's wonderful one-acre farm that I had better set matters straight. I'm McBroom. Josh McBroom. I'll explain about the water-melons in a minute.

I aim to put down the facts, one after the other, the way things happened – exactly.

It began, you might say, the day we left the farm in Connecticut. We piled our youngsters and everything we owned in our old air-cooled Franklin automobile. We headed West.

To count noses, in addition to my own, there was my dear wife Melissa and our eleven red-headed youngsters. Their names were Will*jill*hester*chester*peter*polly*tim*tom* mary*larry*andlittle*clarinda*.

It was summer, and the trees along the way were full of birdsong. We had got as far as Iowa when my dear wife Melissa made a startling discovery. We had *twelve* children along – one too many! She had just counted them again.

I slammed on the brakes and raised a cloud of dust.

'Willjillhesterchesterpeterpollytimtommarylarryand-littleclarinda!' I shouted. 'Line up!'

The youngsters tumbled out of the car. I counted noses and there were twelve. I counted again. Twelve. It was a baffler, as all the faces were familiar. Once more I made the count – but this time I caught Larry slipping around behind. He was having his nose counted twice, and the mystery was solved. The scamp! Didn't we laugh, though, and stretch our legs into the bargain.

Just then a thin, long-legged man came ambling down the road. He was so scrawny I do believe he could have hidden behind a flagpole, ears and all. He wore a tall stiff collar, a diamond pin in his tie, and a straw hat.

'Lost, neighbour?' he asked, spitting out the pips of a green apple he was eating.

'Not a bit,' I said. 'We're heading West, sir. We gave up our farm – it was half rocks and the other half tree-stumps. Folks tell us there's land out West and the sun shines in the winter.'

The stranger pursed his lips. 'You can't beat Iowa for farmland,' he said.

'Maybe so,' I nodded. 'But I'm short of funds. Unless they're giving farms away in Iowa we'll keep a-going.'

The man scratched his chin. 'See here, I've got more land than I can plough. You look like nice folks. I'd like to have you for neighbours. I'll let you have eighty acres cheap. Not a stone or a tree-stump anywhere on the place. Make an offer.'

'Thank you kindly, sir,' I smiled. 'But I'm afraid you would laugh at me if I offered you everything in my leather purse.'

'How much is that?'

'Ten dollars exactly.'

'Sold!' he said.

Well, I almost choked with surprise. I thought he must

be joking, but quick as a flea he was scratching out a deed on the back of an old envelope.

'Hector Jones is my name, neighbour,' he said. 'You can call me Heck – everyone does.'

Was there ever a more kindly and generous man? He signed the deed with a flourish, and I gladly opened the clasp of my purse.

Three milky white moths flew out. They had been gnawing on the ten dollar bill all the way from Connecticut, but enough remained to buy the farm. And not a stone or tree-stump on it!

Mr Heck Jones jumped on the running-board and guided us a mile up the road. My youngsters tried to amuse him along the way. Will wiggled his ears, and Jill crossed her eyes, and Chester twitched his nose like a rabbit, but I reckoned Mr Jones wasn't used to youngsters. Hester flapped her arms like a bird, Peter whistled through his front teeth, which were missing, and Tom tried to stand on his head in the back of the car. Mr Heck Jones ignored them all.

Finally he raised his long arm and pointed.

'There's your property, neighbour,' he said.

Didn't we tumble out of the car in a hurry? We gazed with delight at our new farm. It was broad and sunny, with an oak tree on a gentle hill. There was one defect, to be sure. A boggy-looking pond spread across an acre beside the road. You could lose a cow in a place like that, but we had got a bargain – no doubt about it.

'Mama,' I said to my dear Melissa. 'See that fine old oak on the hill? That's where we'll build our farmhouse.'

'No you won't,' said Mr Heck Jones. 'That oak ain't on your property. All that's yours is what you see under water. Not a rock or a tree-stump in it, like I said.'

I thought he must be having his little joke, except that there wasn't a smile to be found on his face. 'But, *sir*!' I said. 'You clearly stated that the farm was eighty acres.'

'That's right.'

'That marshy pond hardly covers an acre.'

'That's wrong,' he said. 'There are a full eighty acres – one piled on the other, like griddle cakes. I didn't say your farm was all on the surface. It's eighty acres deep, McBroom. Read the deed.'

I read the deed. It was true.

'*Hee-haw! Hee-haw!*' he snorted. 'I got the best of you, McBroom! Good day, neighbour.'

He scurried away, laughing up his sleeve all the way home. I soon learned that Mr Heck was always laughing up his sleeve. Folks told me that when he'd hang up his coat and go to bed, all that stored-up laughter would pour out of his sleeve and keep him awake at nights. But there's no truth to that.

I'll tell you about the water-melons in a minute.

Well, there we stood gazing at our one-acre farm that wasn't good for anything but jumping into on a hot day. And that day was the hottest I could remember. The hottest on record, as it turned out. That was the day, three minutes before noon, when the cornfields all over Iowa exploded into popcorn. That's history. You must have read about that. There are pictures to prove it.

I turned to our children. 'Will*jill*hester*chester*peter-*polly*tim*tom*mary*larry*andlittle*clarinda*,' I said. 'There's always a bright side to things. That pond we bought is a mite muddy but it's wet. Let's jump in and cool off.'

That idea met with favour and we were soon in our swimming togs. I gave the signal, and we took a running

jump. At that moment such a dry spell struck that we
landed in an acre of dry earth. The pond had evaporated.
It was very surprising.

My boys had jumped in head first and there was nothing
to be seen of them but their legs kicking in the air. I had
to pluck them out of the earth like carrots. Some of my girls
were still holding their noses. Of course, they were sorely
disappointed to have that swimming hole pulled out from
under them.

But the moment I ran the topsoil through my fingers,
my farmer's heart skipped a beat. That pond bottom felt

as soft and rich as black silk. 'My dear Melissa!' I called. 'Come look! This topsoil is so rich it ought to be kept in a bank.'

I was in a sudden fever of excitement. That glorious topsoil seemed to cry out for seed. My dear Melissa had a sack of dried beans along, and I sent Will and Chester to fetch it. I saw no need to bother ploughing the field. I directed Polly to draw a straight furrow with a stick and Tim to follow her, poking holes in the ground. Then I came along. I dropped a bean in each hole and stamped on it with my heel.

Well, I had hardly gone a couple of yards when something green and leafy tangled my foot. I looked behind me. There was a beanstalk travelling along in a hurry and looking for a pole to climb on.

'Glory be!' I exclaimed. That soil was *rich*! The stalks were spreading out all over. I had to rush along to keep ahead of them.

By the time I got to the end of the furrow the first stalks had blossomed, and the pods had formed, and they were ready for picking.

You can imagine our excitement. Will's ears wiggled. Jill's eyes crossed. Chester's nose twitched. Hester's arms flapped. Peter's missing front teeth whistled. And Tom stood on his head.

'Willjillhesterchesterpeterpollytimtommarylarryand-littleclarinda,' I shouted. 'Harvest them beans!'

Within an hour we had planted and harvested that entire crop of beans. But was it hot working in the sun! I sent Larry to find a good acorn along the road. We planted it, but it didn't grow near as fast as I had expected. We had to wait an entire three hours for a shade tree.

We made camp under our oak tree, and the next day

we drove to Barnsville with our crop of beans. I traded it for various seeds – carrot and beet and cabbage and other items. The storekeeper found a few kernels of corn that hadn't popped, at the very bottom of the bin.

But we found out that corn was positively dangerous to plant. The stalk shot up so fast it would skin your nose.

Of course, there was a secret to that topsoil. A government man came out and made a study of the matter. He said there had once been a huge lake in that part of Iowa. It had taken thousands of years to shrink up to our pond, as you can imagine. The lake fish must have got packed in worse than sardines. There's nothing like fish to put nitrogen in the soil. That's a scientific fact. Nitrogen makes things grow to beat all. And we did occasionally turn up a fish-bone.

It wasn't long before Mr Heck Jones came round to pay us a neighbourly call. He was eating a raw turnip. When he saw the way we were planting and harvesting cabbage his eyes popped out of his head. It almost cost him his eyesight.

He scurried away, muttering to himself.

'My dear Melissa,' I said. 'That man is up to mischief.'

Folks in town had told me that Mr Heck Jones had the worst farmland in Iowa. He couldn't give it away. Tornado winds had carried off his topsoil and left the hardpan right on top. He had to plough it with wedges and a sledge-hammer. One day we heard a lot of booming on the other side of the hill, and my youngsters went up to see what was happening. It turned out he was planting seeds with a shot-gun.

Meanwhile, we went about our business on the farm. I don't mind saying that before long we were showing a handsome profit. Back in Connecticut we had been lucky to harvest one crop a year. Now we were planting and harvesting three, four crops a *day*.

But there were things we had to be careful about. Weeds, for one thing. My youngsters took turns standing weed guard. The instant a weed popped out of the ground, they'd race to it and hoe it to death. You can imagine what would happen if weeds ever got going in rich soil like ours.

We also had to be careful about planting-time. Once we planted lettuce just before my dear Melissa rang the bell for dinner. While we ate, the lettuce headed up and went to seed. We lost the whole crop.

One day back came Mr Heck Jones with a grin on his face. He had figured out a loop-hole in the deed that made the farm ours.

'*Hee-haw!*' he laughed. He was munching a radish. 'I got the best of you now, Neighbour McBroom. The deed says you were to pay me *everything* in your purse, and you *didn't*.'

'On the contrary, sir,' I answered. 'Ten dollars. There wasn't another cent in my purse.'

'There were *moths* in the purse. I seen 'em flutter out. Three milky white moths, McBroom. I want three moths by three o'clock this afternoon, or I aim to take back the farm. *Hee-haw!*'

And off he went, laughing up his sleeve.

Mama was just ringing the bell for dinner so we didn't have much time. Confound that man! But he did have his legal point. 'Willjillhesterchesterpeterpollytimtommarylarryandlittleclarinda!' I said. 'We've got to catch three milky white moths! Hurry!'

We hurried in all directions. But moths are next to impossible to locate in the day-time. Try it yourself. Each of us came back empty-handed.

My dear Melissa began to cry, for we were sure to lose

our farm. I don't mind telling you that things looked dark. Dark! That was it! I sent the youngsters running down the road to a lonely old pine tree and told them to rush back with a bushel of pine cones.

Didn't we get busy though! We planted a pine cone every three feet. They began to grow. We stood around anxiously, and I kept looking at my pocket watch. I'll tell you about the water-melons in a moment.

Sure enough, by ten minutes to three, those cones had grown into a thick pine forest.

It was dark inside, too! Not a ray of sunlight slipped through the green pine boughs. Deep in the forest I lit a lantern. Hardly a minute passed before I was surrounded by milky white moths – they thought it was night. I caught three on the wing and rushed out of the forest.

There stood Mr Heck Jones with the sheriff.

'*Hee-haw! Hee-haw!*' old Heck laughed. He was eating a quince apple. 'It's nigh on to three o'clock, and you can't catch moths in the day-time. The farm is mine!'
'Not so fast, Neighbour Jones,' said I, with my hands cupped together. 'Here are the three moths. Now, skedaddle, sir, before your feet take root and poison ivy grows out of your ears!'

He scurried away, muttering to himself.

'My dear Melissa,' I said. 'That man is up to mischief. He'll be back.'

It took a good bit of work to clear the timber, I'll tell you. We had some of the pine milled and built ourselves a house on the corner of the farm. What was left we gave away to our neighbours. We were weeks blasting the roots out of the ground.

But I don't want you to think there was nothing but work on our farm. Some crops we grew just for the fun of it. Take pumpkins. The vines grew so fast we could hardly catch the pumpkins. It was something to see. The youngsters used to wear themselves out running after those pumpkins. Sometimes they'd have pumpkin races.

Sunday afternoons, just for the sport of it, the older boys would plant a pumpkin seed and try to catch a ride. It wasn't easy. You had to grab hold the instant the blossom dropped off and the pumpkin began to swell. Whoosh! It would yank you off your feet and take you whizzing over the farm until it wore itself out. Sometimes they'd use banana squash which was faster.

And the girls learned to ride corn stalks like pogo-sticks.

22

It was just a matter of standing over the kernel as the stalk came busting up through the ground. It was good for quite a bounce.

We'd see Mr Heck Jones standing on the hill in the distance, watching. He wasn't going to rest until he had prised us off our land.

Then, late one night, I was awakened by a hee-hawing outside the house. I went to the window and saw old Heck in the moonlight. He was cackling and chuckling and heeing and hawing and sprinkling seed every which way.

I pulled off my sleeping-cap and rushed outside.

'What mischief are you up to, Neighbour Jones!' I shouted.

'*Hee-haw!*' he answered, and scurried away, laughing up his sleeve.

I had a sleepless night, as you can imagine. The next morning, as soon as the sun came up, that farm of ours broke out in weeds. You never saw such weeds! They heaved out of the ground and tumbled madly over each other – chickweed, and milkweed, thistles and wild morning glory. In no time at all the weeds were in a tangle several feet thick and still rising.

We had a fight on our hands, I tell you! 'Willjillhesterchesterpeterpollytimtommarylarryandlittleclarinda!' I shouted. 'There's work to do!'

We started hoeing and hacking away. For every weed we
uprooted, another re-seeded itself. We were a solid month
battling those weeds. If our neighbours hadn't pitched in
to help, we'd still be there burning weeds.

The day finally came when the farm was cleared and
up popped old Heck Jones. He was eating a big slice of
water-melon. That's what I was going to tell you about.

'Howdy, Neighbour McBroom,' he said. 'I came to say
good-bye.'

'Are you leaving, sir?' I asked.

'No, but *you* are.'

I looked him squarely in the eye. 'And if I don't, sir?'

'Why, *hee-haw*, McBroom! There's heaps more of weed seed where that came from!'

My dander was up. I rolled back my sleeves, meaning to give him a whipping he wouldn't forget. But what happened next saved me the bother.

As my youngsters gathered around, Mr Heck Jones made the mistake of spitting out a mouthful of water-melon seeds.

Things did happen fast!

Before I had quite realized what he had done, a water-melon vine whipped up around old Heck's scrawny legs and jerked him off his feet. He went whizzing every which way over the farm. Water-melon seeds were flying. Soon he came zipping back and collided with a pumpkin left over from Sunday. In no time water-melons and pumpkins went galloping all over the place, and they were knocking him about something wild. He streaked here and there. Melons crashed and exploded. Old Heck was so covered with melon pulp he looked like he had been shot out of a sauce bottle.

It was something to see. Will stood there wiggling his ears. Jill crossed her eyes. Chester twitched his nose. Hester flapped her arms like a bird. Peter whistled through his front teeth, which had grown in. Tom stood on his head. And little Clarinda took her first step.

By then the water-melons and pumpkins began to play themselves out. I figured Mr Heck Jones would like to get home as fast as possible. So I asked Larry to fetch me the seed of a large banana.

'*Hee-haw!* Neighbour Jones,' I said, and pitched the seed at his feet. I hardly had time to say good-bye before the vine had him. A long banana squash gave him a fast ride

26

all the way home. I wish you could have been there to see it. He never came back.

That's the entire truth of the matter. Anything else you hear about McBroom's wonderful one-acre farm is an outright fib.

McBROOM AND THE BIG WIND

I CAN'T deny it – it does get a mite windy out here on the prairie. Why, just last year a blow came ripping across our farm and carried off a pail of sweet milk. The next day it came back for the cow.

But that wasn't the howlin', scowlin', all-mighty *big* wind I aim to tell you about. That was just a common little prairie breeze. No account, really. Hardly worth bragging about.

It was the *big* wind that broke my leg. I don't expect you to believe that – yet. I'd best start with some smaller weather and work up to that bone-breaker.

I remember distinctly the first prairie wind that came

28

scampering along after we bought our wonderful one-acre farm. My, that land is rich. Best topsoil in the country. There isn't a thing that won't grow in our rich topsoil, and fast as lightning.

The morning I'm talking about, our oldest boys were helping me to shingle the roof. I had bought a keg of nails, but it turned out those nails were a whit short. We buried them in our wonderful topsoil and watered them down. In five or ten minutes those nails grew a full half-inch.

So there we were, up on the roof, hammering down shingles. There wasn't a cloud in the sky at first. The younger boys were shooting marbles all over the farm and the girls were jumping rope. When I had pounded down the last shingle I said to myself, 'Josh McBroom, that's a mighty stout roof. It'll last a hundred years.'

Just then I felt a small draught on the back of my neck. A moment later one of the girls – it was Polly, as I recall – shouted up to me. 'Pa,' she said, 'do jack rabbits have wings?'

I laughed. 'No, Polly.'

'Then how come there's a flock of jack rabbits flying over the house?'

I looked up. Mercy! Rabbits were flapping their ears across the sky in a perfect V formation, northbound. I knew then we were in for a slight blow.

'Run, everybody!' I shouted to the young 'uns. I didn't want the wind picking them up by the ears. 'Will*jill*-hester*chester*peter*polly*tim*tom*mary*larry*andlittle*clarinda* – in the house! Scamper!'

The clothes-line was already beginning to whip around like a jump rope. My dear wife, Melissa, who had been baking a heap of biscuits, threw open the door. In we dashed and not a moment too soon. The wind was snapping at our heels like a pack of wolves. It aimed to barge right in and make itself at home! A prairie wind has no manners at all.

We slammed the door in its teeth. Now, the wind didn't take that politely. It rammed and battered at the door while all of us pushed and shoved to hold the door shut. My, it was a battle! How the house creaked and trembled!

'Push, my lambs,' I yelled. 'Shove!'

At times the door planks bent like barrel staves. But we held that roaring wind out. When it saw there was no getting past us, the zephyr sneaked around the house to the back door. Howsoever, our oldest boy, Will, was too smart for it. He piled Mama's heap of fresh biscuits against the back door. My dear wife, Melissa, is a wonderful cook, but her biscuits *are* terrible heavy. They made a splendid door-stop.

But what worried me most was our wondrous rich topsoil. That thieving wind was apt to make off with it, leaving us with a trifling hole in the ground.

'Shove, my lambs!' I said. 'Push!'

The battle raged on for an hour. Finally the wind gave up butting its fool head against the door. With a great angry sigh it turned and whisked itself away, scattering fence posts as it went.

We all took a deep breath and I opened the door a crack. Hardly a leaf now stirred on the ground. A bird began to twitter. I rushed outside to our poor one-acre farm.

Mercy! What I saw left me pop-eyed. 'Melissa!' I shouted with glee. 'Willjillhesterchesterpeterpollytimtom-marylarryandlittleclarinda! Come here, my lambs! Look!'

We all gazed in wonder. Our topsoil was still there – every bit. Bless those youngsters! The boys had left their marbles all over the field, and the marbles had grown as large as boulders. There they sat, huge agates and sparkling glassies, holding down our precious topsoil.

But that rambunctious wind didn't leave empty-handed. It ripped off our new shingle roof. Pulled out the nails, too. We found out later the wind had shingled every burrow in the next county.

Now that was a strong draught. But it wasn't a *big* wind. Nothing like the kind that broke my leg. Still, that prairie gust was an education to me.

'Young 'uns,' I said, after we'd rolled those giant marbles down the hill. 'The next uninvited breeze that comes along, we'll be ready for it. There are two sides to every flapjack. It appears to me the wind can be downright useful on our farm if we let it know who's boss.'

The next gusty day that came along, we put it to work for us. I made a wind plough. I rigged a bed-sheet and tackle to our old farm plough. Soon as a breeze sprung up I'd go tacking to and fro over the farm, ploughing as I went. Our son Chester once ploughed the entire farm in under three minutes.

On Thanksgiving morning Mama told the girls to pluck a large turkey for dinner. They didn't much like that chore, but a prairie gust arrived just in time. The girls stuck the turkey out of the window. The wind plucked that turkey clean, feathers and all.

Oh, we got downright glad to see a blow come along. The young 'uns were always wanting to go out and play in the wind, but Mama was afraid they'd be carried off. So I made them wind-shoes – made 'em out of heavy iron skillets. Out in the breeze those shoes felt light as feathers. The girls would jump rope with the clothes-line. The wind spun the rope, of course.

Many a time I saw the youngsters put on their wind-shoes and go clumping outside with a big tin funnel and all the empty bottles and jugs they could round up. They'd cork the containers jam-full of prairie wind.

Then, come summer, when there wasn't a breath of air, they'd uncork a bottle or two of fresh winter wind and enjoy the cool breeze.

Of course, we had to wind-proof the farm every fall. We'd plant the field in buttercups. My, they were slippery – all that butter, I guess. The wind would slip and slide over the farm without being able to get a purchase of the topsoil. By then the boys and I had re-shingled the roof. We used screws instead of nails.

Mercy! Then came the *big* wind!

It started out gently enough. There were a few jack rabbits and some crows flying backwards through the air. Nothing out of the ordinary.

Of course the girls went outside to jump the clothes-line and the boys got busy laying up the bottles of wind for summer. Mama had just baked a batch of fresh biscuits. My, they did smell good! I ate a dozen or so hot out of the oven. And that turned out to be a terrible mistake.

Outside, the wind was picking up ground speed and scattering fence posts as it went.

'Willjillhesterchesterpeterpollytimtommarylarryand-littleclarinda!' I shouted. 'Inside, my lambs. That wind is getting ornery!'

The young 'uns came trooping in and pulled off their wind-shoes. And not a moment too soon. The clothes-line began to whip around so fast it seemed to disappear. Then we saw a hen-house come flying through the air, with the hens still in it.

The sky was turning dark and mean. The wind came out of the far north, howling and shrieking and shaking the house. In the cupboard, cups chattered in their saucers.

Soon we noticed big balls of fur rolling along the prairie like tumbleweeds. Turned out they were timber wolves from up north. And then an old hollow log came spinning across the farm and split against my chopping-stump. Out rolled a black bear, and was he in a temper! He had been trying to hibernate and didn't take kindly to being awakened. He gave out a roar and looked around for some-body to chase. He saw us at the windows and decided we would do.

The mere sight of him scared the young 'uns and they huddled together, holding hands, near the fireplace.

I got down my shotgun and opened a window. That was a *mistake*! Two things happened at once. The bear was coming on and in my haste I forgot to calculate the direction of the wind. It came shrieking along the side of the house and when I poked the gun-barrel out of the window, well, the wind bent it like an angle iron. That

33

buck-shot flew due south. I found out later it brought down a brace of ducks over Mexico.

But worse than that, when I threw open the window such a draught came in that our young 'uns *were sucked up through the chimney*! Holding hands, they were carried away like a string of sausages.

Mama near fainted away. 'My dear Melissa,' I exclaimed. 'Don't you worry! I'll get our young 'uns back!'

I fetched a rope and rushed outside. I could see the young 'uns up in the sky and blowing south.

I could also see the bear and he could see me. He gave a growl with a mouthful of teeth like rusty nails. He rose up on his hind-legs and came towards me with his eyes glowing red as fire.

I didn't fancy tangling with that monster. I dodged around behind the clothes-line. I kept one eye on the bear and the other on the young 'uns. They were now flying away over the county and hardly looked bigger than May-flies.

The bear charged towards me. The wind was spinning the clothes-line so fast he couldn't see it. And he charged smack into it. My, didn't he begin to jump! He jumped red-hot pepper, only faster. He had got himself trapped inside the rope and couldn't jump out.

Of course, I didn't lose a moment. I began flapping my arms like a bird. That was such an enormous *big* wind I figured I could fly after the young 'uns. The wind tugged and pulled at me, but it couldn't lift me an inch off the ground.

Tarnation! I had eaten too many biscuits. They were heavy as lead and weighed me down.

The young 'uns were almost out of sight. I rushed to the barn for the wind-plough. Once out in the breeze, the bed-

sheet filled with wind. Off I shot like a cannon-ball, ploughing a deep furrow as I went.

Didn't I streak along, though! I was making better time than the young 'uns. I kept my hands on the plough handles and steered around barns and farmhouses. I saw hay-stacks explode in the wind. If that wind got any

stronger it wouldn't surprise me to see the sun blown off course. It would set in the south at high noon.

I ploughed right along and gained rapidly on the young 'uns. They were still holding hands and just clearing the tree-tops. Before long I was within hailing distance.

'Be brave, my lambs,' I shouted. 'Hold tight!'

I spurted after them until their shadows lay across my path. But the bed-sheet was so swelled out with wind that I couldn't stop the plough. Before I could let go of the handles and jump off I had sailed far *ahead* of the young 'uns.

I heaved the rope into the air. 'Willjillhesterchesterpeterpollytimtommarylarryandlittleclarinda!' I shouted as they came flying overhead. 'Hang on!'

Hester missed the rope, and Jill missed the rope, and so did Peter. But Will caught it. I had to dig my heels in the earth to hold them. And then I started back. The young 'uns were too light for the wind. They hung in the air. I had to drag them home on the rope like balloons on a string.

Of course it took most of the day to shoulder my way back through the wind. It was a mighty struggle, I tell you! It was near supper-time when we saw our farmhouse ahead, and that black bear was still jumping rope!

I dragged the young 'uns into the house. The rascals! They had had a jolly time flying through the air, and wanted to do it again! Mama put them to bed with their wind-shoes on.

The wind blew all night, and the next morning that bear was still jumping rope. His tongue was hanging out and he had lost so much weight he was skin and bones.

Finally, about mid-morning, the wind got tired of blowing one way, so it blew the other. We got to feeling sorry for that bear and cut him loose. He was so tuckered out he didn't even growl. He just pointed himself towards the tall timber to find another hollow log to crawl into. But he had lost the fine art of walking. We watched him jump, jump, jump north until he was out of sight.

That was the howlin', scowlin', all-mighty *big* wind that broke my leg. It had not only pulled up fence posts, but the *holes* as well. It dropped one of those holes right outside the barn door and I stepped in it.

That's the bottom truth. Everyone on the prairie knows Josh McBroom would rather break his leg than tell a fib.

McBROOM'S EAR

GRASSHOPPERS – yes, they did get wind of our wonderful one-acre farm. The long-legged, saw-legged, hop-legged rascals ate us out of house and home.

You know how grasshoppers are. They'd as soon spit tobacco juice as look at you. And they're terrible hungry creatures. I guess there's nothing that can eat more in less time than a swarm of grasshoppers. Green things, especially, make their mouths water.

I don't intend to talk about it with a hee and a haw. Mercy, no! If you know me – Josh McBroom – you know I'd as soon live in a tree as tamper with the truth.

I'd best start with the weather. Summer was just waking up, but the days weren't near warm enough yet for grasshoppers. The young 'uns were helping me to dig a water-well. They talked of growing one thing and another to enter in the County Fair.

I guess you've heard how amazing rich our farm was. Anything would grow in it – quick. Seeds would burst in the ground and crops would shoot right up before your eyes. Why, just yesterday our oldest boy dropped a five-cent piece and before he could find it that nickel had grown to a quarter.

Early one morning a skinny, tangle-haired stranger came ambling along the road. My, he was tall! I do believe if his hat fell off it would take a day or two to reach the ground.

'Howdy, sir,' he said. 'I'm Slim-Face John from here, there, and other places. I'll paint your barn cheap.'

That man was not only tall, skinny, and tangle-haired, he was near-sighted. 'We don't own a barn,' I said.

He squinted and laughed. 'In that case,' he said, 'I'll paint it free.'

'Done,' I smiled.

He painted that no-barn in less than a second, with time left over. He appeared to be hungry, so my dear wife, Melissa, gave him a hearty breakfast and he went ambling away. 'I'll be back.' He waved.

The young 'uns and I kept digging that well. My, it was hard work. They'd lower a bucket, I'd fill it with earth, and they'd haul it up like a tug-of-war. All eleven of them.

The days grew longer and hotter. Flies began to drop out of the air with sun-stroke.

But it still wasn't grasshopper weather.

'Will*jill*hester*chester*peter*polly*tim*tom*mary*larry*and-little*clarinda*!' I had to shout from the bottom of the well. 'Work to do! Haul up the bucket!'

'Aw, Pa,' Chester complained from the tree-house. 'I'm fixin' to grow a prize water-melon for the Fair. A fifty-pounder.'

'I think I'll grow a pumpkin,' Polly said.

'Well, I'm growing impatient!' I said. 'Haul up the bucket, my lambs, and dump it. County Fair's still a week off.'

The next day was a real sizzler. At high noon the yellow wax beans began melting on the vines. They dripped like candles.

No – it wasn't grasshopper weather yet. The leggy creatures would catch cold on a chilly day like that.

We finished the well at last, with the bucketfuls of earth standing in a big heap beside it. Along about supper-time that tall, skinny, tangle-haired, near-sighted stranger was back.

'Howdy,' he said. 'I'm Slim-Face John from here, there, and other places. I'll dig you a water-well cheap.'

'We've got a well,' I said.

'In that case,' he answered, 'I'll dig it free.'

He stayed for supper and then went ambling away. 'I'll be back.' He waved.

Another day passed. The sun-ball began to outdo itself. Hot? Why, the next morning it was so infernal hot that a block of ice felt warm to the touch. Mama had to boil water to cool it off. Sunflowers along the road picked up their roots and hurried under the trees for shade.

That was grasshopper weather.

Just after breakfast the first jumpers arrived. They came in twos and fours. Our farm stood green as an emerald and it was bound to catch their eye. Before long they were turning up in sixes and eights.

I must admit those first visitors surprised us with their nice table manners. They didn't spit tobacco juice any which way. Peter set out an old coffee can and they used it for a spittoon.

By noon hop-legs were arriving by the fifties and hundreds. They nibbled our cabbage and lettuce, but it was nothing to be alarmed about. We could grow vegetables faster than they could eat them – three or four crops a day.

Along about sundown the saw-legged visitors came whirring in by the hundreds and the thousands. I wasn't worried. Grasshoppers are hardly worth counting in small numbers like that.

'Pa,' Chester said at breakfast. 'County Fair's tomorrow. Reckon it's time to set out my water-melons.'

'I'm going to grow a prize tomato,' Mary declared. 'Big as a balloon.'

'You young 'uns use the patch behind the house,' I said. 'I aim to plant the farm in corn.'

The grasshoppers didn't get in our way. Larry and little Clarinda fed them turnip greens out of their hands. I got the field planted in no time.

My, it was fine corn-growing weather. The stalks leapt right up, dangling with ears.

Suddenly a silvery green cloud rose off the horizon and raced towards us.

Grasshoppers!

Grasshoppers by the thousands! Grasshoppers by the millions! Little did we know it was the beginning of the Great Grasshopper War – or, as it came to be called, the War of McBroom's Ear.

'Will*jill*hester*chester*peter*polly*tim*tom*mary*larry*and-little*clarinda*!' I shouted. 'Brooms and branches! Shoo them off!'

We began yelling and running about and waving our weapons. The grasshoppers spun over our ripening corn-field. They feasted their eyes – and flew off.

'We – scared 'em away!' Tim declared.

'No,' I said. 'That was just the advance party. They went back for the main herd. *And here they come!*'

Acres of grasshoppers! Square miles of grasshoppers! They came streaking towards us like a great roaring thunderbolt of war.

'Brooms and branches!' I yelled.

The hungry devils tucked napkins under their chins and swooped down for the attack. Mercy! The air got so thick with hoppers you could swing a bucket once and fill it twice. They made a whirring, hopping, jumping fog. We could barely see a foot beyond our noses.

But we could hear the ravenous rascals. They were chomping and chewing up our cornfield and spitting out the cobs. They ate that farm right down to the ground in exactly four seconds flat.

Then they rose in the air, still hungry as wolves, and waited for the next crop.

'Pa!' Chester said. 'They skinned my water-melons!'

'Pa!' Mary cried. 'They didn't even wait for my tomatoes to ripen. They ate them green!'

'Pa!' little Clarinda said. 'What happened to your socks?'

I looked down. Glory be! Those infernal dinner guests had eaten the socks right out of my shoes – green socks. All they left were the holes in the toes.

Some of the young 'uns broke into tears. 'We won't be able to grow anything for the County Fair!'

'We're not beat yet, my lambs,' I said, thinking as hard as I could. 'Those hoppers did have us outnumbered, but not outsmarted. I'm going to town for seed. Better clear away the corn-cobs.'

I drove to town in our air-cooled Franklin automobile and was back before noon with fifty pounds of fine seed. The grasshoppers were still stretched all over the sky, waiting. The young 'uns had cleared the farm, throwing the corn-cobs on the heap of dirt beside the well.

'Not a moment to lose,' I said. 'Help scatter the seed.'

Before long our farm was bushed out, green as a one-acre jungle. Those hoppers smacked their lips and fought to get at it. They whirred and swarmed and craned and crunched – that crop disappeared as if sucked up by a tornado.

Well, you should have seen how surprised they were! That first wave of hoppers was all but breathing fire. And no wonder. They had dined on hot green peppers.

They streaked off in a hurry, looking for something to drink.

Of course, there were still tons of grasshoppers left. We kept sowing crops of hot green peppers all afternoon until there wasn't a jump-leg to be seen. We found out later they had swarmed to a lake in the next county and drunk it dry.

But they'd be back. The young 'uns would have to grow their prizewinners in a hurry.

'Pa – look!' little Clarinda shouted.

She was pointing to the tall heap of dirt, littered with corncobs. Glory be! The grasshoppers had missed a lone kernel and it had taken root behind our backs. A cornstalk was growing up as big as a tree.

That dirt hill was powerful rich. The roots of that wondrous stalk were having a banquet! A single ear of corn began to form before our eyes. Big? Why, it was already fatter than a pot-bellied stove and still growing.

'That looks like a prizewinner to me!' I declared. 'You scamps will go partners.'

Jill and Hester and Polly climbed to their tree-house to keep a sharp eye out for the grasshoppers. That ear of corn grew longer and fatter. It was a beauty! The stalk began to bend under its weight. And it was ripening fast.

Didn't we get busy, though! We fixed loops of rope around that ear so as to let it down easy. Will climbed up a ladder with a bucksaw and went to work. It must have taken him five minutes to saw that giant ear off the stalk.

We eased it down with the ropes. I tell you, we could hardly believe our eyes. That ear of corn was so big you couldn't see it in a single glance. You had to look twice.

'Grasshoppers!' Jill shouted from the tree-house. 'Grasshoppers coming, Pa!'

'Quick,' I said. 'Into the house!'

It took all of us to lift that ear of corn. But it

wouldn't fit through the door. And it wouldn't fit through the window.

'The well!' I shouted.

We lowered it by ropes and covered the well over with some rusty sheets of corrugated tin. And just in time. Those hoppers had spotted our great ear from the sky and came whirring across the farm in a green blizzard. But they couldn't get at that ear of corn.

'It's safe for the night,' I said.

'How will we *ever* get it past the hoppers to the Fair tomorrow?' Mary asked.

I don't have to tell you the problem gave me a sleepless night. About four in the morning I jumped out of bed and woke the young 'uns.

'Brooms and buckets!' I said. 'Follow me.'

We tiptoed outside, careful not to wake the jump-legs. We quietly raised our ear of corn from the well and replaced the sheets of corrugated tin. Then I filled the buckets from the shed.

'Start painting,' I whispered.

The young 'uns dipped their brooms and painted that giant ear from end to end and all over.

At sun-up the grasshoppers rose from the fields and went looking for breakfast. They headed straight for the well, banging their heads on the rusty tin. My, what a clatter! They thought our enormous big ear was still down there.

Well, it was in plain sight. Only they didn't recognize it. The husk wasn't green any more. We had *whitewashed* it.

We lifted it to the roof of the old Franklin and tied it down. 'Everybody pile in.' I smiled, starting up the motor. 'We're off to the Fair!'

Just then Mr Slim-Face John came along.

'Howdy.' He smiled. 'I'll paint your farmhouse cheap.'

'Oh, I'd dearly like that,' Mama said. 'Red, with white window-sills.'

'Done,' I said. 'You'll find paint in the shed.' And we were off.

Well, you should have seen heads turn along the way. What *was* that thing on the roof of our car? An ear of corn? No sir! No farmer can raise corn that big. And white as chalk!

We bumped along the dirt road, following signs to the County Fair. We enjoyed the sights – barns, and silos, and cows chewing their cuds in the shade.

'How much farther?' Polly asked.

'Ten, twelve miles,' I said. 'Be patient.'

I noticed the prairie windmills begin to turn. A hot wind was coming up, dragging a cloud with it. We could hear the rumble of thunder.

'How much farther, Pa?' Tim asked.

'Eight, ten miles,' I said. 'Be patient.'

But I didn't like the look of that cloud. It grew darker and heavier and came blowing our way.

'Heads in!' I called to the young 'uns. 'Thunder shower ahead.'

We met the storm head on. It didn't amount to much, but those raindrops were almost hot enough to scald you. They bounced like sparks off the hood. A moment later the sky was blue again and the summer shower behind us.

'How much farther, Pa?' Mary asked.

'Six, eight miles,' I said. 'Be patient.'

'Pa,' Will said. He hadn't bothered to pull his head in out of the window and his hair was wet. 'Pa, look what's happened to our corn!'

I jammed on the brakes and got out to see. Lo and

47

behold – the husk was bright green again! The summer
shower had washed off the whitewash.

I jumped back behind the wheel and off we spun.
'Watch for grasshoppers,' I shouted.

'I'm watching, Pa,' little Clarinda answered. '*And here
they come!*'

Well, it was a race. The hoppers came roaring after us in
full battle formation. The old Franklin creaked and
groaned and clanked, but her heart was in it. We bumped
in and out of the ruts and jumped a few.

'They're gaining on us, Pa!'

I had the foot pedal to the floorboard. Soon we could see
the flags and banners of the County Fair ahead.

But not seen enough. The first hop-legs were landing on
the roof and we could hear them ripping and tearing at the
husk. By the time we reached the fairgrounds we'd have
nothing left but the cob.

But the old Franklin started to back-fire, banging and

booming something fierce. Those hop-legs jumped a mile and we made it across the fairgrounds.

I charged right into the main-exhibition building and jammed on the brakes. 'Shut all the doors!' I shouted. 'Grasshoppers! Grasshoppers coming!'

The doors swung shut and we could breathe easy at last. Folks began to cluster around, their eyes rising as their jaws fell open at the wonder of our ear of corn. And I declare if the hungry rascals hadn't husked it neat as you please.

We lifted it down off the roof and put it on display on two picnic tables. The judges came by and asked what name to enter it by.

'McBroom.' I smiled. 'Will*jill*hester*chester*peter*polly*-tim*tom*mary*larry*andlittle*clarinda* – McBroom!'

Well, the judges gave it first, second, third prize and honourable mention, too. But, my, it was getting over-heated in there with the doors closed.

The young 'uns lined up to have their picture taken for the county paper. There was one long smile reaching from Will at one end to little Clarinda at the other. The noon sun kept beating down on the roof and of a sudden there came a loud bang.

I thought at first it was our tired old Franklin. But no. It was the young 'uns' enormous, big prize-winning ear of corn – beginning to pop! The inside of the building had grown so infernal hot it was a perfect popcorn popper.

Well, it did get noisy in there! Kernels swelled and exploded like great white cannon-balls. They bounced off the roof and the walls. Pop-pop-pop. Pop. Pop-pop-pop-pop-pop! Folks ducked and others ran. Corn in their rows boomed away in regular broadsides! I tell you popcorn was flying all over the hall and piling up like a heavy snow-fall. Pop-pop-pop-pop-pop-pop-pop-pop! In no time at

49

all we were buried in light, fluffy popcorn. It swelled to the roof and forced open the doors. It overflowed the building at both ends.

There wasn't a grasshopper left in sight. All that ruckus had sent them flying. As far as I know they headed for the full moon. Must have heard it was made of green cheese. We never saw them again.

We stayed the afternoon – everyone did. Folks melted up buckets of prize butter and someone went to town for barrels of salt. There was more than enough fresh popcorn to go round. Salted and buttered, it was delicious. One piece was enough to feed an entire family.

Did I tell you I'd as soon live in a tree as tamper with the truth? Well, when we got back that night we found our farmhouse chawed and gnawed and eaten to the ground. Mr Slim-Face John was not only tall, skinny, tangle-haired, and near-sighted. He was also colour-blind. Painted our house green.

Yes – it's a mite crowded living up here in the young 'uns' tree-house. But those prize ribbons – they're all mighty nice to look at.

McBROOM'S GHOST

GHOSTS? Mercy, yes – I can tell you a thing or three about ghosts. As sure as my name's Josh McBroom a haunt came lurking about our wonderful one-acre farm.

I don't know when that confounded dry-bones first moved in with us, but I suspicion it was when we built our new home. Then winter set in. An *uncommon* cold winter it was, too, though not so cold that an honest man would tell fibs about it. Still, you had to be careful when you lit a match. The flame would freeze and you had to wait for a thaw to blow it out.

Some old-timers declared that was just a middling cold winter out here on the prairie. Nothing for the record books. Still, we did lose our rooster, Sillibub. He jumped on the woodpile, opened his beak to crow the break of day and the poor thing quick-froze as stiff as glass.

The way I reckoned it, that ghost was whisking about and got ice-bound on our farm.

The young 'uns were the first to discover the pesky creature. A March thaw had come along and they had gone outside to play. I was bundled up in bed with the laryngitis – hadn't been able to speak above a whisper for three days. I passed the time listening to John Philip Sousa's band on our talking-machine. My, those piccolos did sound pretty!

Suddenly, the young 'uns were back and they appeared kind of strange in the eyes.

'Pa,' said our youngest boy, Larry. 'Pa, do roosters ever turn into ghosts?'

I tried to clear my throat. 'Never heard of such a thing,' I croaked.

'But we just this minute heard old Sillibub *crow*,' said our oldest girl, Jill.

'Impossible, my lambs,' I whispered, and they went out to frolic in the sun again.

I cranked up the talking-machine and once more Mr Sousa's band came marching and trilling out of the morning-glory horn. Suddenly the young 'uns were back – all eleven of them.

'We heard it again,' said Will.

'*Cock-a-doodle-do!*' little Clarinda crowed. 'Plain as day, Pa. Out by the woodpile.'

I shook my head. 'Must be Mr Sousa's piccolos you're hearing,' I said hoarsely, and they went out to play again.

I cranked up the machine and before I knew it the young 'uns came flocking back in.

'Yes, Pa?' Will said.

'Yes, Pa?' Jill said.

'You called, Pa?' Hester said.

I lifted the needle off the record and gazed at them. 'Called?' I croaked. Then I laughed hoarsely. 'Why, you scamps know I can't raise my voice above a whisper. Aren't you full of mischief today!'

'But we *heard* you, Pa,' Chester said.

' "Will*jill*hester*chester*peter*polly*tim*tom*mary*larry*and-little*clarinda*!" ' Polly said. 'It was your very own voice, Pa. And plain as day.'

Well, after that they wouldn't go back out to play. They were certain some scaresome thing was roving about. Sure enough, the next morning we were awakened at dawn by the crowing of a rooster. It *did* sound like old Sillibub. But I said, 'Heck Jones must have got himself a rooster. That's what we hear.'

'But Heck Jones doesn't keep chickens,' my dear wife Melissa reminded me. 'You know he's raising hogs, Pa. The meanest, wildest hogs I ever saw. I do believe he hopes they'll root up our farm and drive us out.'

Heck Jones was our neighbour, and an almighty torment to us. He was tall and scrawny and just as mean and ornery as those Arkansas razorback hogs of his. He'd tried more than once to get our rich one-acre farm for himself.

It wouldn't surprise me if he was making those queer noises himself. Well, if he thought he could scare us off our property he was mistaken!

By the time I got over the laryngitis the young 'uns were afraid to leave the house. They just stared out the windows. Something was out there. They were certain of it.

So I bundled up and marched outside to look for Heck Jones' footprints in the mud. Well, I had hardly got as far as the woodpile when a voice came ripping out of the still air.

'Will*jill*hester*chester*peter*polly*tim*tom*mary*larry*and-little*clarinda*!'

That voice sounded *exactly* like my own. I spun about. But there wasn't a soul to be seen.

I don't mind admitting that my hair shot up on end. It knocked my hat off.

There wasn't a footprint to be seen, either.

'Do you think the farm is haunted?' Larry asked.

'No,' I answered firmly. 'Haunts clank chains and moan like the wind and rap at doors.'

Just then there came a rap at the door. The young 'uns all shot looks at me – Mama too.

Well, I got up and opened the door and there was no one there. That's when I had to admit there was a dry-bones dodging about our property. And mercy, what a sly,

prankster creature it was! When that ghost wasn't mimicking old Sillibub it was mimicking me.

Well, we didn't sleep very well after that. Some nights I didn't sleep at all. I kept a sharp eye out for that haunt, but it never would show itself.

Finally, Mama and the young 'uns began to talk about giving up the farm. Then we had another freeze and for three solid weeks that spirit didn't make a sound. We reckoned it had moved away.

We breathed easier, I can tell you! There was no more talk of leaving the farm. The young 'uns passed the time leafing through the mail order catalogue and we all listened to the talking-machine.

'Pa, we'd dearly love to have a dog,' Jill said one day.

'You won't find dogs in the mail order catalogue, my lambs,' I said.

'We know, Pa,' said Chester. 'But can't we have a dog? A big, shaggy farm dog?'

I shook my head sadly. A dog would be the ruination of

our amazing rich one-acre farm. There was nothing that wouldn't grow in that remarkable soil of ours – and quicker'n scat. I thought back to the summer day little Clarinda had lost a baby tooth. By the time we found it that tooth had grown so large we had to put up a block and tackle to extract it.

'No,' I said. 'Dogs dig holes and bury bones. Those bones would grow the size of buried logs. I'm sorry, my lambs.'

The icicles began to melt in the spring thaw – and there came another knock at the door.

The haunt was back!

That night the young 'uns slept huddled together all in one bed. Didn't I pace the floor, though! That door-rapping, rooster-crowing, me-mimicking dry-bones would drive us off our farm. Unless I drove it off first.

Early the next morning I trudged through the mud to town. Everyone said that the Widow Witherbee was a ghost seer.

I called on her first thing. She was a spry little cricket of a lady who bought and sold hand-me-down clothes. But tarnation! Her eyesight was failing and she said she couldn't spy out ghosts any more.

'What am I to do?' I asked, as a litter of mongrel pups nipped at my ankles.

'Simple,' the Widow Witherbee said. 'Burn a pile of old shoes. Never fails to drive ghosts away.'

Well, that sounded like twaddle to me, but I was desperate. She went poking through rags and old clothes and I bought all the worn-out, hand-me-down shoes she could find.

'You'll also need a dog,' she said.

My eyebrows shot up. 'A dog?'

'Certainly,' she said. 'Certainly. How are you going to know if you ran off that haunt without a dog? Hounds can see ghosts. Mongrels are best. When their ears stand up and they freeze and point like a bird dog – you know they're staring straight at a ghost. Then you have to burn more shoes.'

So I bought one of her flop-eared pups and started back for the farm, carrying a bushel basket of old shoes. As I approached the house I could see the young 'uns' faces at the windows. Piccolos were trilling merrily in the air.

But dash it all! When I opened the door I saw that no one had a record on the talking-machine.

'Confound that haunt!' I exploded. 'Now it's imitating John Philip Sousa's entire marching band!'

Of course, the young 'uns couldn't believe I had brought home a dog. It was the first time all winter long I saw smiles on their faces. Didn't they gather around him, though! They promised to keep close watch so that he wouldn't bury any bones.

I didn't lose much time burning that bushel of old shoes. Mercy, what an infernal strong smell! I could imagine that dry-bones holding its nose and rattling away, never to return.

Every day after that we walked the pup around the farm and never once did he raise his flop-ears and point.

'By ginger!' I exclaimed finally. 'The old shoes did it. That haunt is gone!'

By that time the young 'uns had decided on a name for the pup. They called him Zip. He grew to be the handiest farm dog I ever saw. That rich soil of ours was rarin' to go and we started our spring planting – raised a crop of tomatoes and two crops of carrots the first day. In no time at all the young 'uns taught Zip to dig a furrow. Straight as a beeline, too!

But our troubles weren't over with that ghost chased off. One burning hot morning we planted the farm in corn. The stalks came busting up through the ground, leafing out and dangling with ears. I tell you, Heck Jones' hogs acted as if we had rung the dinner bell. Mercy! They came roaring down on us in a snorting, squealing, thundering herd.

'Will*jill*hester*chester*peter*polly*tim*tom*mary*larry*and-little*clarinda*!' I shouted. '*And* Zip! Run for your lives!'

Those hungry, half-wild razorback hogs broke down the stalks and gorged themselves on sweet ears of corn. Then they rooted up the farm looking for left-over carrots.

Well, those razorbacks finally trotted home, with their stomachs scraping the ground, and I followed along behind.

'Heck Jones,' I said. He was standing in a cloud of flies and eating a shoofly pie. It was mostly made of molasses and brown sugar, which attracted the flies and kept a body busy shooing them off. 'Heck Jones, it appears to me you've been starving your hogs.'

'Bless my soul, they don't look starved to me,' he chuckled, shooing flies off his shoofly pie. 'See for yourself, neighbour.'

'Heck Jones,' I said stoutly. 'If you aim to raise hogs I'd advise you to grow your own hog feed.'

'No need for that, neighbour,' he laughed. 'There's plenty of feed about and razorbacks can fend for themselves. Of course, if you hanker to give up farming I might make an offer for that patch of ground you're working.'

'Heck Jones,' I said for the last time. I could hardly see him for the cloud of flies. 'You're mistaken if you think you and your razorbacks can drive us off, sir. Either pen up those hogs or I'll have the law on you!'

'There's no law says I've got to pen my hogs,' he said, finishing off the pie and a few flies into the bargain. 'Anyway, neighbour, no pen would hold the rascals.'

Well, I'll admit he was right about that. We fenced our farm, but those infernal hogs busted through it and scattered the pieces like a cyclone. We strung barbed-wire. It only stopped them long enough to scratch their backs. Barbed wire was a *comfort* to those razorbacks.

I tell you we battled those hogs all spring and summer. We planted a crop of prickly pear cactus, but not even that kept the herd out. They ate the pears and picked their teeth with the prickly spines.

All the while Heck Jones stood on the brow of the hill eating shoofly pie and going, 'Hee-*haw*! Hee-*haw*!' His hogs grew fatter and fatter. I tell you we were lucky to save enough food for our own table.

Another growing season like that and we'd be ruined!

Then summer came to an end and we knew we were in for more than an uncommon cold winter. It was going to be a *dreadful* cold winter. There were signs.

I remember that the boys had gone fishing in late October and brought home a catfish. *That catfish had grown a coat of winter fur.*

That wasn't all. After the first fall of snow, the young 'uns built a snowman. The next morning it was gone. We found out later that snowman had gone *south* for the winter.

Well, it turned out to be the Winter of the Big Freeze. I don't intend to stray from the facts, but I distinctly remember one day Polly dropped her comb on the floor and when she picked it up the teeth were chattering.

As things turned out, that was just a middling cold day in the Winter of the Big Freeze. The temperature kept dropping and I must admit some downright *unusual* things began to happen.

For one thing smoke took to freezing in the chimney. I had to blast it out with a shotgun three times a day. And we couldn't sit down to a bowl of Mama's hot soup before a crust of ice formed on top. The girls used to set the table with a knife, a fork, a spoon – and an ice-pick.

Well, the temperature kept dropping, but we didn't complain. At least there was no ghost lurking about and Heck Jones' hogs stayed home and the young 'uns had the dog to play with. I kept cranking the talking-machine.

Then the *big* freeze set in. Red barns for miles around turned blue with the cold. There's many an eye-witness to that!

One day the temperature fell so low that sunlight froze on the ground.

Now, I disbelieved that myself. So I scooped up a chunk in a frying-pan and brought it inside. Sure enough, I was able to read to the young 'uns that night by the glow of that frozen chunk of winter sun.

Of course, we had our share of wolves about. Many a night, through the windows, we could see great packs of them trying their best to howl. I suspicioned laryngitis. Those wolves couldn't make a sound. It was pitiful.

Well, spring thaw came at last. I remember stepping outside and the first thing I heard was a voice.

'Hee-*haw*!'

'What mischief are you up to now, Heck Jones?' I answered back.

But as I looked about me I saw there wasn't another soul on the farm.

Then I knew. My hair rose, knocking my hat to the ground again. That door-rapping, rooster-crowing, me-mimicking, hee-*hawing* ghost was back!

'Zip!' I shouted, and we went tracking all over the farm. Voices popped up behind us and in front of us and across the woodpile.

But that dog of ours never once lifted his flop-ears.

'Confound it!' I grumbled to Mama and the young 'uns. 'Zip can't see ghosts at all!'

The poor mongrel knew I was dreadful disappointed in him. He lit out through my legs and dug a straight furrow in the farm quick as I ever saw. When that didn't bring a smile to my face, he zipped over to the corn bin and took a cob in his mouth. He'd watched us plant many a time. He ran back up the furrow, shelling the corn with his teeth and planting the kernels with a poke of his nose.

'Maybe Zip can't see ghosts,' Will said. 'But he's a powerful smart farm dog, Pa. Can't we still keep him?'

I didn't have a moment to answer. As the cornstalks shot up, Heck Jones appeared eating a shoofly pie on the rim of the hill. At the same instant his razorback hogs came thundering towards us – and that infernal haunt began trilling like a piccolo.

'Run for your lives!' I shouted.

We all ran but Zip. The corn was ripening fast and he meant to *harvest* it.

I started back out-of-doors to snatch him up, but suddenly that prankish ghost changed its tune. It began howling like a pack of hungry wolves.

You never heard such a howling! And didn't those hogs stop in their tracks! I tell you they near jumped out of their skins. That ghost kept yipping and howling from every quarter. Heck Jones didn't have a chance to *hee* and to *haw*. Those razorbacks turned on their heels. They trampled him in the mud and kept running – though one of them did come back for the shoofly pie. My, they did run! I heard later they didn't stop until they arrived back in Arkansas where they were mistaken for guinea pigs. They had run off that much weight.

'Yes, my lambs,' I said to the young 'uns. 'Reckon we'll keep ol' Zip. Look at him harvest that corn!'

Well, we'd got rid of Heck Jones' razorback hogs, but we still had that dry-bones cutting up. The young 'uns remembered to be scared and streaked behind closed doors.

I stood my ground, scratching my head. Sounds were

breaking out everywhere in the air. As if howling and yipping like an entire pack of wolves wasn't enough, that haunt joined in with Mr Sousa's entire marching band. I must admit it had those piccolos down perfect.

I kept scratching my head and suddenly I said to myself, 'Why, there's no haunt around here. No wonder ol' Zip couldn't spy it out.'

Glory be! It was clear to me now. There never *had* been a haunt lurking about. It was nothing but the weather playing pranks on us. No wonder we hadn't been able to hear wolves in the dead of winter. *The sounds had frozen.*

And now all those sounds were *thawing* out!

Well, it wasn't long before I coaxed the young 'uns outside again, and soon they were enjoying the rappings at the door and the yips of wolves and shotgun blasts three times a day from the chimney-top.

And didn't they laugh about Heck Jones' razorback hogs running from the howling and yipping of last winter's wolves!

Well, that's the truth about our prairie winters and McBroom's ghost – as sure as I'm a truthful man.

HERE COMES
M^cBROOM!

HERE COMES McBROOM!

CONTENTS

M^cBROOM TELLS A LIE

It's true – I did tell a lie once.

I don't mean the summer nights we hung caged chickens in the farmhouse for lanterns. Those hens had eaten so many lightning bugs they glowed brighter'n kerosene lamps.

And I don't mean the cold snap that came along so sudden that blazing sunshine froze to the ground. We pick-axed chunks of it for the stove to cook on.

That's the genuine truth, sure and certain as my name's Josh McBroom.

The time I told a lie – well, I'd best start with the spring day the young 'uns came home from school. They were lugging an old black stovepipe, which they put in the barn.

The next day they dragged home a broken buggy wheel. They put that in the barn, too.

Gracious! It wasn't long before that barn was filling up with empty coffee cans, scrap pieces of lumber, tin funnels, busted chairs, a rusted bicycle and all manner of throw-away stuff.

Then they began a-sawing and a-hammering and hardly came out of the barn to eat. They were building a secret something-or-other. The scamps kept it covered with a sheet. I reckoned they'd tell us when they were ready.

'Will*jill*hester*chester*peter*polly*tim*tom*mary*larry*and-little*clarinda*!' my dear wife Melissa had to call out every evening. 'Supper!'

We had hardly sat down to eat when Jill asked, 'Pa, would Mexican jumping beans grow on our farm?'

I hadn't seen anything yet that wouldn't grow on our wonderful one-acre farm. That trifling patch of earth was so amazing rich we could plant and harvest two-three crops a day – with time left over for a game of horseshoes. Why, just last month Little Clarinda dropped her silver engraved baby fork and by the time we found it the thing had grown into a silver engraved pitchfork.

'Mexican jumping beans?' I answered. 'I don't think they make good eating.'

'We don't want them to eat,' Will said.

'Will you let us grow a crop?' Polly asked. 'We need bushels and bushels of 'em.'

'For our invention,' Tom put in.

'In that case,' I smiled, 'jump to it, my lambs.'

They traded with a boy at school who owned a jar of the hopping beans. First thing Saturday morning they lit out the back door to plant their crop.

And along came our foxy-eyed neighbour, Heck Jones. You never saw such a spare-ribbed and rattle-boned man. Why, he was so skinny he could slip through a knot-hole without tipping his hat. He wore a diamond stickpin in his tie and was swinging a bamboo cane. Our dog, Zip, stood barking at him.

'Josh McBroom,' he said. 'I'm here to do some trading.'

'Trade what?'

'My big farm for yours – even. You can keep the dog.'

'No sir and nohow,' I said. His farm was so worn out that he had to plant his own weeds.

He leaned both hands heavily on his bamboo cane. '*Hee-haw!*' he snickered. 'Reckon I'll get your land, neighbour – one way or t'other.'

And off he ambled up the road, *hee-hawing* through his nose. He'd been visiting almighty often lately. I stomped over the hole his cane had left in the ground. I had to be careful not to let holes get a good start in our rich topsoil – the blamed things grow.

Meanwhile the young 'uns had laid out the rows and began sowing the beans.

Well, that was a mistake. I should have known that our soil was too powerful strong for jumping beans. The seeds sprouted faster'n the twitch of a sheep's tail and those Mexican bushes shot up lickety-bang. As they quick-

73

dried in the prairie sun the pods began to shake and rattle and Chester shouted, 'Pa, look!'

Merciful powers! Those buzzing, jumping, wiggle-waggling pods jerked the roots clear out of the ground. And off those bushes went, leaping and hopping every which way.

'Willjillhesterchesterpeterpollytimtommarylarryand-littleclarinda!' I called out. 'After them, my lambs!'

Didn't those plants lead us a merry chase! A good many got clean away, hopping and bucking and rattling across the countryside. But we did manage to capture enough for the young 'uns' invention.

They were shelling the beans when the dog reared up barking. Heck Jones was back with four scrawny hens and a bobtailed rooster out for a walk.

'Howdy, neighbour,' he said. 'I'm here to do some trading. My farm for yours and I'll throw in this flock of fat hens. My prize rooster, too. You can keep the dog.'

I looked at those sorry fowl, scratching and pecking away in the dirt. 'No sir and nohow,' I said. 'Our farm's not for trade, Heck Jones.'

'*Hee-haw*, I'll get it one way or t'other,' he said, tipping

his hat towards the end of his nose. 'Good day, neighbour.'

It was the next morning, before breakfast, when the young 'uns finished tinkering with their invention. They called my dear wife Melissa and me out to the barn and whipped off the sheet.

Glory be! There stood an odds and ends contraption on four wheels. A rain barrel was mounted in front with three tin funnels sticking out of the top. The scamps had fixed up their collection of broken chairs to seat all eleven of them.

'We're going to call it a Jumping Beanmobile,' Jill said.

'If it runs we won't have to walk all that five miles to school and back,' said Peter.

'My stars,' Mama declared.

'Pile in, everybody,' Will said, 'and let's start 'er up.'

The young 'uns flocked to their seats. Will, Jill and Hester began pouring beans into the funnels.

Mercy! You never heard such a racket inside that rain barrel. The beans began to hop, jump and leap something fearful, bouncing against tin cans from the sound of things. I found out later the cans were fitted into stovepipe – something like the cylinders on my broken-down Franklin automobile. They had things hooked up to the front wheels with bicycle chains.

'More fuel!' Will called out, and more beans went down the funnels.

I declare. The next moment the Jumping Beanmobile clanked forward – a full inch.

'More beans!' Polly shouted happily.

But tarnation! The barrel was already so hopping full that beans were leaping like fleas out of the tops of the funnels.

The young 'uns sat there with the smiles dropping from their faces, one by one.

'A splendid invention, my lambs,' I said. 'Why, all you need is a stronger fuel.'

'*Hee-haw*.' Heck Jones had come up behind us and was helping himself to the water dipper. 'That infernal machine'll never run, neighbours. Make good firewood, though.'

The young 'uns rolled their Jumping Beanmobile back into the barn. I was feeling mighty low for them, the way Heck Jones made fun of them. He was cackling so that he spilled most of the dipper of water on his shoes.

'McBroom, you drive a hard bargain. I'll trade you my farm, a flock of fat hens, my prize rooster and two plump hogs. You can keep your farm dog.'

Plump? Those hogs of his were so puny they could hide behind a broomstick.

'No sir and nohow,' I said.

'I'll get what I'm after one way or t'other,' he *hee-hawed*, and ambled out of sight around the barn.

When the young 'uns came in to breakfast they said they'd seen him scraping the mud off his shoes into an old flour sack.

'By thunder!' I exclaimed. 'That's why the confounded rascal's been paying us so many visits.'

The older young 'uns were standing at the stove breaking fresh eggs into skillets. 'Pa – there's something wrong with these breakfast eggs,' said Will.

But I was hardly listening. 'Why, Heck Jones doesn't intend to trade for our farm,' I declared.

'Pa, come look,' said Jill from the stove.

'Valuable as gold dust, our topsoil. And he's been stealing it! Yup, out of that hollow bamboo cane he pokes in the earth. And off his wet shoes. And out of the craws of the chickens he brings along to peck dirt!'

'Pa – come quick, but stand back!' my dear wife Melissa exclaimed.

I hopped to the stove as she broke another fresh egg into the skillet. Why, soon as it was fried on one side that egg jumped up in the air. It flipped over and landed on the other side to fry.

'Well, don't that beat all,' I said. 'The hens must have been eating your Mexican jumping beans. Yup, and they're laying eggs that *flip* themselves. An amazing invention, my lambs!'

But they wouldn't be cheered up by the flip-flopping eggs. A gloom was on them because they wouldn't be riding to school in their Beanmobile.

I scratched my head most of the day. It wouldn't do any good to fence the farm to keep Heck Jones off. You might as well put up a windbreak out of chicken wire.

The young 'uns were still feeling almighty low and downsome at supper when my dear wife Melissa tried to jolly everybody up. 'Let's pop some corn.'

Well, a strange look came over all those sad faces. 'Popcorn,' Jill whispered.

'Popcorn!' said Hester, beginning to smile.

'POPCORN!' Will laughed. 'Bet that'll run our machine!'

Didn't those kids light out for the barn in a hurry! In no time at all they were clanking and hammering to turn the Beanmobile into a Popcornmobile.

They were still at it the next day, after school, when Heck Jones came running with his shoes off. I reckoned he planned to steal pinches of our farm between his toes.

'I'll have the law on you, McBroom!'

Egg was dripping off his nose and chin. 'Do tell,' I said coldly.

'You grew them jumping beans, didn't you?'

'Best ever. Looks like your hens pecked 'em down and you didn't step back from the egg skillet fast enough.'

'Hang them blasted eggs. Look there at my blue ribbon cow, Princess Prunella!'

My eyes near shot out of my head. There on the horizon that stupid, worthless cow of his was leaping and high-jumping and bucking.

'Kicked a hole right through the barn roof!' Heck Jones snorted. 'You allowed them dangerous bushes of yours to get loose and now Princess Prunella's stomachs are full of jumping beans – all four of 'em!'

'Didn't know she was royalty,' I said. 'Got her name changed kind of sudden, didn't she?'

'That cow's ruined. It would take ten men on ladders to try and milk her. Worth a fortune, Princess Prunella was, with all her blue ribbons.'

I knew for a fact that dumb cow hadn't won a ribbon in her life – but she did eat several once at the County Fair.

'Reckon I'll have to shoot her before she does any more damage,' he said, beginning to dab at his eyes. 'Poor creature.'

Well, all that dabbing didn't fool me. He could peel an acre of onions without dropping a tear. But I reckoned I was responsible for all the mischief, letting those bushes get away from us.

'Sir,' I said. 'If you'll guarantee not to set foot on this farm I'll pay for a barn roof. And I'll buy that ignorant cow from you. I reckon when she settles down she'll give churned butter for a month. Mighty valuable now, Prunella is.'

'She ain't for sale!' Heck Jones snapped. 'Don't think you're going to slip out so light and easy. I intend to see you in jail, McBroom! Farming with intent to poison up my livestock with crazy-beans. Unless –'

'I'm listening, sir.'

He cleared his throat. 'Neighbour, I'm a kindly man. If you want to trade farms we'll call it fair and square.'

'Well, no sir and nohow,' I said. 'And if I weren't a kindly man I'd have the sheriff after you for trying to steal our topsoil, trifle by trifle.'

He caught his hat as a wind sprang up and flapped his coat-tails.

'Slander, sir! I'll have the law on you double. Anyway, you can't prove it!'

'Why, the proof is right between your toes.'

He looked down at his feet. 'Dear, dear me,' he grinned. 'I declare if I wasn't in such a rush I forgot my shoes.'

'And your hollow bamboo cane.'

'Well now, neighbour, we ought to be able to settle things between ourselves.' He lifted his thin nose into the wind – that man could sniff things miles off. 'Why, you just grow me a crop of tomatoes to make up for my barn roof and we'll forget the rest.'

'I'll deliver 'em before supper.'

'No, neighbour. Can't use 'em yet. Gotta find a buyer at a good price.' He whipped out a pencil and a piece of paper. 'I'll just write out the agreement. Best to do things honest and legal. You deliver the tomatoes when I say so – fresh off the vine, mind you – and I'll guarantee not to set foot on your farm again.'

Glory be! We'd be rid of the petty scoundrel at last.

'But fair's fair, McBroom. I'm entitled to a guarantee too. I'll just put down that if you don't live up to the

bargain – why, this useless, worn-out one-acre farm is mine. Sign here.'

Useless? Worn-out? My pride rose up and arched like a cat's back. I could raise a crop of tomatoes in an hour. The *hee-haw* would be on him. I signed.

'And no more skulking around, sir,' I said.

'A bargain's a bargain,' he nodded solemnly. But as he ambled off I thought I heard him snicker through his nose.

It was about sunset when the young 'uns rolled their Popcornmobile out of the barn. 'It's finished, Pa,' Will said.

They had attached black tin stovepipe underneath the floorboards with bailing wire. It made a mighty stout-looking exhaust pipe.

'And look, Pa,' Larry said. 'We got headlights, just like your broken-down Franklin.'

Indeed, they did! Two quart canning jars were fixed to the front. And the scamps had filled the jars with lightning bugs!

'Pa,' Mary said. 'Can we have a chunk of frozen sunlight out of the icehouse?'

'Not much left,' I replied. 'But help yourself.'

By early candlelight they had dropped a clod of sunlight in the barrel together with a dozen ears of corn. They piled into the seats and waited for the sunshine to thaw and pop the corn and start the machinery clanking.

My dear wife Melissa hurried out to take the sheets off the line – the prairie wind was turning a mite gritty – and there stood Heck Jones.

'Evenin', neighbours,' he said. There was a tricksy look in his eye and a piece of paper in his hand. 'McBroom, you guaranteed to deliver a crop of tomatoes on demand. Well, I'm demanding 'em *now*.'

My eyebrows jumped. 'Drat it, you can see the sun's down!' I declared.

'There's nothing about the sun in the contract. You read it.'

'And it's going to kick up a dust storm before long.'

'Nothing in the contract about a dust storm. You signed it.'

'Sir, you expect me to grow you a crop of tomatoes *at night in a dust storm*?'

83

'*Hee-haw*, neighbour. If you don't, this farm's mine. I'll give you till sun-up. Not a moment later, McBroom!'

And off he went, chuckling and snickering and *hee-hawing* through his nose.

'Oh, Pa,' my dear wife Melissa cried. Even the young 'uns were getting a mite onion-eyed.

My heart had sunk somewhere down around my socks, only lower. 'Tarnation!' I said. 'That rascal's slippery as an eel dipped in lard.'

Just then the corn began popping like firecrackers inside the young 'uns' rain barrel.

'Pa, we're moving!' Jill exclaimed.

Sure enough, the chunk of frozen sunlight had thawed out and the corn was exploding from the stored-up heat.

I tried to raise a smile. Will grabbed the steering-wheel tight and began driving the young 'uns around the barn. Popcorn shot out of the exhaust pipe, white as snow.

We didn't have enough of that frozen sunshine left to grow a crop, worse luck! But when I saw those two head-lights coming around the barn my heart leaped back in place. The jars full of fireflies lit up the way like it was high noon!

'Willjillhesterchesterpeterpollymarylarryandlittle-clarinda!' I shouted. 'Fetch canning jars. Fill 'em up with lightning bugs. Quick, my lambs. Not a moment to waste.'

The Popcornmobile sputtered to a stop, spitting out the last corn-cobs from the tailpipe.

Chester said, 'The critters have got kind of scarce around here, Pa.'

'The thickest place is way the other side of Heck Jones' place,' Mary said.

'At Seven-Mile Meadow,' Polly nodded.

'A powerful long walk,' said Larry.

'Who said anything about walking?' I laughed. 'You've got your Popcornmobile, haven't you?'

Didn't we get busy! The young 'uns fetched all the canning jars in the cellar and bushels of corn for fuel. With a fresh chunk of frozen sunshine in the barrel, off they took – spraying popcorn behind them.

I set to work planting tomato seeds. It was full dark, but I could see fine. My dear wife Melissa held up a chicken by the feet – one of those lantern-glowing hens I was telling you about.

Then I began pounding stakes in the ground for the tomatoes to climb up. It was slow work with the wind blowing grit in my eyes.

'I do hope the young 'uns don't get lost,' my dear wife Melissa said. 'It's going to blow a real dust storm by morning.'

'Heck Jones had sniffed it coming,' I declared. 'But lost? Not our scamps. I can hear 'em now. And see 'em too – look!'

They were still a long way off but those headlights glowed, bright as sunrise. And that Popcornmobile sounded like the Fourth of July, loud enough to wake snakes.

Jill had taken a turn at the wheel and steered towards the barn. All the kids were waving and laughing. I reckoned that was the best ride they'd ever had.

'That's a Jim Dandy machine you built,' I smiled. 'And I see you found a lightning bug or two.'

'Thicker'n mosquitoes, over at Seven-Mile Meadow,' Polly said.

Well, it didn't take long to hang those jars of fireflies on the tomato stakes. And glory be! They lit up the farm bright as day.

It wasn't a moment before the tomato sprouts came busting up through the earth. They broke into leaf and the vines started towards those canning jars. I do believe they preferred that home-made sunshine! In fact, before we could harvest the crop, pull the stakes and plug the holes a good many of those tomatoes got sunscald!

We loaded up the Popcornmobile with bushel baskets of tomatoes and I fetched one of the last chunks of frozen sunshine from the icehouse. Will threw a dozen ears of corn into the engine and I went along for the ride.

We made so many trips to Heck Jones' place the popcorn piled up along the road like a snowbank. Finally, minutes before dawn, I hammered at the door.

'Wake up, Heck Jones!' I called.

'*Hee-haw!*' He began to laugh so hard you'd think he'd swallowed a feather duster. He opened the door and stood there in his nightcap, the legal paper in his hand.

'Told you I'd get your farm one way or t'other, McBroom! It's dawn by the clock and that powerful rich, git-up-and-git acre is all mine!'

'Yup, it's dawn,' I said. 'No arguing that, Heck Jones. And there's my end of the bargain.'

When he saw that crop of tomatoes he just about swallowed his teeth. His mouth puckered up tighter'n bark on a tree.

I took the legal paper out of his hand. 'And you bargained to stay off our useless, worn-out one-acre farm, sir. With your hollow cane and your chickens and your muddy shoes and your curled toes. Good day, Mr Jones.'

The young 'uns and I all piled into the Popcornmobile to start for home. That's when I saw Princess Prunella. Only she wasn't jumping any more.

'Merciful powers!' I declared. 'Look there! That numskull cow mistook all this popcorn for snow and has froze to death!'

We got home for a big breakfast and just in time. That prairie dust storm rolled in and stayed for weeks on end. My, it was thick, that dust. Before long our dog was chasing rabbits *up* their burrows. The rodents had dug their holes in the air.

And Heck Jones didn't have any more sense than to climb up on his barn roof and start shingling over the holes Princess Prunella had made. He couldn't see what he was doing until the wind took a shift and the dust cleared. That's when he saw he'd nailed shingles eight feet out in the dust. They all came tumbling down, but he didn't get hurt. Fell into the tomatoes.

Now it's true – I did tell a lie once. That cow of his didn't *really* freeze to death in all that popcorn. But she did catch a terrible cold.

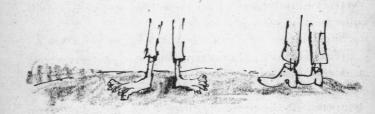

McBROOM THE RAINMAKER

I DISLIKE to tell you this, but some folks have no regard for the truth. A stranger claims he was riding a mule past our wonderful one-acre farm and was attacked by wood-peckers.

Well, there's no truth to that. No, indeed! Those weren't woodpeckers. They were common prairie mos-quitoes.

Small ones.

Why, skeeters grow so large out here that everybody uses chicken wire for mosquito netting. But I'm not going to say an unkind word about those zing-zanging, hot-tempered, needle-nosed creatures. They rescued our farm from ruin. That was during the Big Drought we had last year.

Dry? Merciful powers! Our young 'uns found some polliwogs and had to teach them to swim. It hadn't rained in so long those tadpoles had never seen water.

That's the sworn truth — certain as my name's Josh McBroom. Why, I'd as soon grab a skunk by the tail as tell a falsehood.

Now, I'd best creep up on the Big Drought the way it crept up on us. I remember we did our spring ploughing,

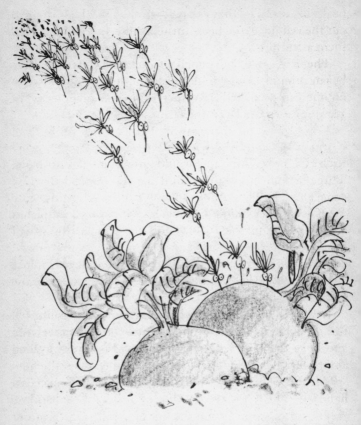

as usual, and the skeeters hatched out as usual. The blood-sucking rapscallions could be mighty pesky, but we'd learned to distract them. The thirsty critters would drink up *anything* red.

'Will*jill*hester*chester*peter*polly*tim*tom*mary*larry*and-little*clarinda*!' I called out. 'I hear the whine of gallinippers. Better put in a patch of beets.'

Once the beets were up the skeeters stuck in their long

beaks like straws. Didn't they feast, though! They drained out the red juice, the beets turned white and we harvested them as turnips.

The first sign of a dry spell coming was when our clocks began running slow. I don't mean the store-bought kind – no one can predict the weather with a tin timepiece. We grew our own clocks on the farm. Vegetable clocks.

Now, I'll admit that may be hard to believe, but not if you understand the remarkable nature of our topsoil. Rich? Glory be! Anything would grow in it – lickety-bang. Three or four crops a day until the confounded Big Dry came along.

Of course, we didn't grow clocks with gears and springs and a name on the dial. Came close once, though. I dropped my dollar pocket-watch one day and before I could find it the thing had put down roots and grown into a three-dollar alarm clock. But it never kept accurate time after that.

It was our young 'uns who discovered they could tell the time by vegetables. They planted a cucumber seed and once the vine leaped out of the ground it travelled along steady as a clock.

'An inch a second,' Will said. 'Kind of like a second hand.'

'Blossoms come out on the minute,' Jill said. 'Kind of like a minute hand.'

They tried other vegetable timepieces, but pole beans had a way of running a mite fast and squash a mite slow.

As I say, those homegrown clocks began running down. I remember my dear wife Melissa was boiling three-and-a-half-minute eggs for breakfast. Little Clarinda planted a cucumber seed and before it grew three blossoms and thirty inches those eggs were hard-boiled.

'Mercy!' I declared. 'Topsoil must be drying out.'

But I wasn't worried. Rain would turn up.

What turned up was our neighbour, Heck Jones. Rusty nails stuck out of his bulging pockets. He was a tall, scrawny man with eyes shifty as minnows. '*Hee-haw!*' he laughed. 'Drought's a-comin'. You won't be able to grow weeds. Better buy some of my rain nails.'

'Rain nails?' I said.

'Magnetized 'em myself,' he grinned. 'Secret formula, neighbour. Pound 'em in the ground and they'll draw rain clouds like flies to a garbage heap.'

'Fiddle-faddle,' I declared. 'Flapdoodle, sir!'

'Why, only five dollars apiece. I'm trying to be of service, neighbour. Other farmers'll buy my rain nails – *hee-haw!*' And off he went, cackling through his nose.

Wasn't he an infernal scoundrel, I thought! Setting out to swindle his neighbours into buying rusty old nails at five dollars each!

Well, the days turned drier and drier. No doubt about it – our wonderful topsoil was losing some of its get-up-

and-go. Why, it took almost a whole day to raise a crop of corn. The young 'uns had planted a plum tree, but all it would grow was prunes. Dogs would fight over a dry bone – for the moisture in it.

'Willjillhesterchesterpeterpollytimtommarylarryand-littleclarinda!' I called. 'Keep your eyes peeled for rain.'

They took turns in the tree-house scanning the skies, and one night Chester said, 'Pa, what if it doesn't rain by Fourth of July? How'll we shoot off firecrackers?'

'Be patient, my lambs,' I said. We used to grow our own firecrackers, too. Don't let me forget to tell you about it. 'Why, it's a long spell to Fourth of July.'

My, wasn't the next morning a scorcher! The sun came out so hot that our hens laid fried eggs. But no, that wasn't the Big Dry. The young 'uns planted water-melons to cool off and beets to keep the mosquitoes away.

'Look!' Polly exclaimed, pointing to the water-melons. 'Pa, they're rising off the ground!'

Rising? They began to float in the air like balloons! We could hardly believe our eyes. And gracious me! When we cut those melons open it turned out they were full of hot air.

'*Hee-haw!*' Heck Jones laughed. There he stood jingling the rusty nails in his pocket. 'Better buy some rain nails. Only ten dollars apiece.'

I shot him a scowl. 'You've doubled the price, sir.'

'True, neighbour. And the weather's double as dry. Big Drought's a-comin' – it's almost here. How many ten-dollar rain nails do you want?'

'Flim-flam!' I answered stoutly. 'None, sir!'

And off he went, cackling through his nose. Drought wasn't a worry to him. Heck Jones was such a shiftless farmer that he could carry a whole year's harvest in a tin

93

cup. Now he was making himself rich peddling flim-flam, flapdoodle, fiddle-faddle rain attractors. Farmers all over the county were hammering those useless, rusty old nails into the ground. They were getting desperate.

Well, I was getting a mite worried myself. Our beets were growing smaller and smaller and the skeeters were growing larger and larger. Many a time, before dawn, a rapping at the windows would wake us out of a sound sleep. It was those confounded, needle-nosed gallinippers pecking away, demanding breakfast.

Then it came – the Big Dry.

Mercy! Our cow began giving powdered milk. We pumped away on our water pump, but all it brought up was dry steam. The oldest boys went fishing and caught six dried catfish.

'Not a rain cloud in sight, Pa,' Mary called from the tree-house.

'Watch out for gallinippers!' Larry shouted, as a mosquito made a dive at him. The earth was so parched we couldn't raise a crop of beets and the varmints were getting downright vicious. Then, as I stood there, I felt my shoes getting tighter and tighter.

'Thunderation!' I exclaimed. 'Our topsoil's gone in reverse. It's *shrinking* things.'

Didn't I lay awake for most of the night! Our wonderful one-acre farm might shrink to a square foot. And all night long the skeeters rattled the windows and hammered at the door. Big? The *smallest* ones must have weighed three pounds. In the moonlight I saw them chase a yellow-billed cuckoo.

Didn't that make me sit up in a hurry! An idea struck me. Glory be! I'd break that drought.

First thing in the morning I took Will and Chester to

town with me and rented three wagons and a bird-cage. We drove straight home and I called everyone together.

'Shovels, my lambs! Heap these wagons full of topsoil!'

But Larry and little Clarinda were still worried about Fourth of July. 'We won't be able to grow fireworks, Pa!'

'You have my word,' I declared firmly.

The mosquitoes were rising in swarms, growing more temperish by the hour.

'Shovel, my lambs!' I said. 'Fill the wagons!'

I heard a cackling sound and there stood Heck Jones. '*Hee-haw*, neighbour. Clearing out? Giving up? Why, I've got three rain nails left. Last chance.'

'Sir,' I said. 'Your rusty old nails are a bamboozle and a hornswoggle. I intend to do a bit of rainmaking and break this drought!'

'*Hee-haw!*' he laughed, and ambled off.

Before long we were on our way. I drove the first wagon, with the young 'uns following along behind in the other two. It might be a longish trip and we had loaded up with picnic hampers of food. We also brought along rolls of chicken wire and our raincoats.

'Where are we going, Pa?' Jill called from the wagon behind.

'Hunting.'

'Hunting?' Tom said.

'Exactly, my lambs. We're going to track down a rain cloud.'

'But how, Pa?' asked Tim.

I lifted the bird-cage from under the wagon seat. 'Presto,' I said, and whipped off the cover. 'Look at that lost-looking, scared-looking, long-tailed creature. Found it hiding from the skeeters under a milk pail this morning. It's a genuine rain crow, my lambs.'

96

'A rain crow?' Mary said. 'It doesn't look like a crow at all.'

'Correct and exactly,' I said, smiling. 'It looks like a yellow-billed cuckoo and that's what it is. But don't folks call 'em rain crows? Why, that bird can smell a downpour coming sixty miles away. Rattles its throat and begins to squawk. All we got to do is follow that squawk.'

But you never heard such a quiet bird! We travelled miles and miles across the prairie, this way and the other, and not a rattle out of that rain crow.

The Big Dry had done its mischief everywhere. We didn't see a dog without his tongue dragging, and it took two of them to bark at us once. A farmer told us he hadn't been able to grow anything all year but baked potatoes! We came to a field of molasses cane and our wagon wheels almost got stuck fast. I thought at first we had run over chewing-gum. But no – that sweet cane had melted down to molasses and was dripping across the road.

Of course, we slept under chicken wire – covered the horses too. My, what a racket the gallinippers made!

Day after day we hauled our three loads of topsoil across the prairie, but that rain crow didn't so much as clear its throat.

The young 'uns were getting impatient. 'Speak up, rain crow,' Chester muttered desperately.

'Rattle,' Hester pleaded.

'Squawk,' said Peter.

'Please,' said Mary. 'Just a little peep would help.'

Not a cloud appeared in the sky. I'll confess I was getting a mite discouraged. And the Fourth of July not another two weeks off!

We curled up under chicken wire that night, as usual, and the big skeeters kept banging into it so you could hardly sleep. Rattled like a hailstorm. And suddenly, at daybreak, I rose up laughing.

'Hear that?'

The young 'uns crowded around the rain crow. We hadn't been able to hear its voice rattle for the mosquitoes. Now it turned in its cage, gazed off to the north-west, opened its yellow beak and let out a real, ear-busting rain cry.

'K-*kawk*! K-*kawk*! K-*kawk*!'

'Put on your raincoats, my lambs!' I said and we rushed to the wagons.

'K-*kawk*! K-*kawk*! K-*kawk*!'

Didn't we raise dust! That bird faced north-west like a dog on point. There was a rain cloud out there and before long Jill gave a shout.

'I see it!'

And the others chimed in one after the other. 'Me, too!'

'K-*kawk*! K-*kawk*! K-*kawk*!'

We headed directly for that lone cloud, the young 'uns yelling, the horses snorting and the bird squawking.

Glory be! The first raindrops spattered as large as quarters. And my, didn't the young 'uns frolic in that cloudburst! They lifted their faces and opened their mouths and drank right out of the sky. They splashed about and felt mud between their toes for the first time in ages. We all forgot to put on our raincoats and got wet as fish.

Our dried-up topsoil soaked up raindrops like a sponge. It was a joy to behold! But if we stayed longer we'd get stuck in the mud.

'Back in the wagons!' I shouted. 'Home, my lambs, and not a moment to lose.'

Well, home was right where we left it and so was Heck Jones. He was fixing to give his house a fresh coat of paint – I reckoned with the money he'd got selling rusty nails. He'd even bought himself a mosquito-proof suit of armour, and was clanking around in it. Many a skeeter bent its stinger trying to drill into that tin suit.

He lifted the steel visor. 'Howdy, neighbour. Come back to put your farm up for sale? I'll make you a generous offer. A nickle an acre.'

'Preposterous, sir!' I answered, my temper rising.

'Why, farmers all over the county are ready to sell out if this drought doesn't break in twenty-four hours. Five cents an acre – that's my top price, neighbour.'

'Our farm is not for sale,' I declared. 'And the drought is about over. I'm going to make rain.'

'*Hee-haw!*' he cackled. 'The Big Drought's only half of it. You don't see any skeeters, do you? But they'll be back and you'll wish you had a suit of armour, same as me. They chased the blacksmith out of his shop. Yup, and they're busy sharpening their noses on his grindstone. Sell, neighbour, and run for your lives.'

'Never, sir,' I answered. But I did rush my dear wife Melissa and the young 'uns into the house. Then I got a pinch of onion seeds and went from wagon to wagon, sewing a few seeds in each load of moist earth. I didn't want to crowd those onions.

Now, that rich topsoil of ours had been idle a long time – it was rarin' to go. Before I could run back to the house the greens were up. By the time I could get down my shotgun the tops had grown four or five feet tall – onions are terrible slow growers. Before I could load my shotgun the bulbs were finally busting up through the soil.

We stood at the windows watching. Those onion roots were having a great feast. The wagons heaved and creaked as the onions swelled and lifted themselves – they were already the size of pumpkins. But that wasn't near big enough. Soon they were larger'n washtubs and began to shoulder the smaller ones off the wagons.

Suddenly we heard a distant roaring in the air. Those

zing-zanging, hot-tempered, blood-sucking prairie mosquitoes were returning from town with their stingers
freshly sharpened. The Big Dry hadn't done their disposi-
tions any good – their tempers were at a boil.

'You going to shoot them down, Pa?' Will asked.

'Too many for that,' I answered.

'How big do those onions have to grow?' Chester asked.

'How big are they now?'

'A little smaller'n a cow shed.'

'That's big enough,' I nodded, lifting the window just
enough to poke the shotgun through.

Well, the gallinippers spied the onions – I had planted
red onions, you know – and came swarming over our farm.
I let go at the bulbs with a double charge of buckshot and
slammed the window.

'Handkerchiefs, everyone!' I called out. The odour of

fresh-cut onion
shot through the air,
under the door and through
the cracks. Cry? In no time our
handkerchiefs were wet as dish-rags.

Well! You never saw such surprised gallinippers. They zing-zanged every which way, most of them backwards. And weep? Their eyes began to flow like sprinkling cans. Onion tears! The roof began to leak. Mud puddles formed everywhere. Before long the downpour was equal to any cloudburst I ever saw. Near flooded our farm!

The skeeters kept their distance after that. But they'd been mighty helpful.

With our farm freshly watered we grew tons of great onions – three or four crops a day. Gave them away to farmers all over the county.

The newspaper ran a picture of the whole family – the rain crow, too.

McBROOM THE RAINMAKER BREAKS BIG DROUGHT

We didn't hear a *hee* or a *haw* out of Heck Jones. Inside his clanking suit of armour he grumbled and growled and finished painting his house. And that was a mistake, for the gallinippers hadn't left the county. They had just flocked off somewhere for a breath of fresh air.

Well, they flocked back. I was standing with my shoes in the earth. My feet had been a torment ever since our dry topsoil had shrunk the leather.

'Little Clarinda,' I said. 'Kindly plant a vegetable clock. I reckon it'll take one minute exactly to grow these shoes two sizes larger.'

She planted a cucumber seed – and that's when the gallinippers returned. Flocks and flocks of them and, my, didn't they look hungry! You could see their ribs standing out. They headed for Heck Jones' house as if he'd rung the dinner-bell. That infernal, wily neighbour of ours had painted his house a fool-headed red.

Well! The huge skeeters dropped like hawks. They speared the wood siding with their long, grindstone-sharpened stingers. Must have gone clear through, for we could see Heck Jones in the windows, hammering the tips of the spears close against the wall.

Oh, he was chuckling and cackling. The gallinippers flapped their wings like caught roosters. Thousands of them! The next thing I knew all those flapping wings lifted the house a few inches. Then a foot. I was surprised to see the floor remain behind – I reckoned Heck Jones had pulled the nails to sell. Then those prairie mosquitoes gave a mighty heave – and flew off. With the house.

Little Clarinda and I were so dumbfounded we'd forgot about the cucumber clock! It had grown thirty-seven blossoms. I tripped over my own feet, and no wonder! My shoes had grown more'n a yard long.

'K-*kawk*! K-*kawk*! K-*kawk*!'

Glory be! Rain – and it wasn't long in coming. I almost felt sorry for Heck Jones. He could be seen walking the floor without a roof over his head in the downpour. Of course, that suit of armour shed water and kept him dry. It also rusted in all its joints. He'd be wearing it still if we hadn't pitched in with can-openers to get him out.

The young 'uns had a splendid Fourth of July. Grew all the fireworks they wanted. They'd dash about with bean shooters – shooting radish seeds into the ground. You know how fast radishes come up. In our rich topsoil they grew quicker'n the eye. The seeds hardly touched the

ground before they took root and swelled up and exploded. They'd go off like strings of firecrackers.

And, mercy, what a racket! At nightfall a scared cat ran up a tree and I went up a ladder to get it down. Reached in the branches and caught it by the tail.

I'd be lying if I didn't admit the truth. It was a skunk.

MᶜBROOM'S ZOO

BEASTS and birds? Oh, I've heard some whoppers about the strange critters out here on the prairie. Why, just the other day a fellow told me he'd once owned a talking rattlesnake. It didn't *talk*, exactly. He said it shook its rattles in Morse code.

Well, there's not an ounce of fact in that. Gracious, no! That fellow had no regard for the truth. Everyone knows that a snake can't spell.

But yes, we did collect some mighty peculiar and surprising animals here on our wonderful one-acre farm. It's not generally known that we had the only Great Hidebehind in captivity. I must not forget to tell you about it.

If you've been reading about me – Josh McBroom – you'll know that I'm a stickler for the honest facts. Why, I'd rather sit on a porcupine than tell a fib.

Of course, there are beasts and birds that come and go with the weather, so I'd best start with that ill-tempered spring morning. A low, ashy-looking cloud stretched from one horizon to the other, and the air was quiet. *Uncom-*

monly quiet. Not a note of birdsong to be heard. But I paid it no mind and we planted our farm in tomatoes.

I reckon you know about that astonishing rich topsoil of ours. My, it was a wonder! There was nothing you couldn't grow on our farm and quicker'n lickety-whoop. Why, just last Wednesday one of the young 'uns left a hand trowel stuck in the ground and by morning it had grown into a shovel.

But to get back to those tomatoes. It wasn't five minutes before the vines were winding up the wood stakes and putting out yellow blossoms. Soon our one-acre farm was weighted down with green tomatoes. As they swelled up and reddened we had to work fast before the stakes took root.

'Will*jill*hester*chester*peter*polly*tim*tom*mary*larry*and-little*clarinda*!' I called to the young 'uns. 'Time to harvest the crop. Looks like thirty tons, at least!'

'And look what's coming, Pa!' Little Clarinda shouted. She pointed off towards the north-west and I about jumped out of my shoes. There appeared to be a stout black rope dangling from the clouds in the distance. 'Tornado!' I yelled. 'Into the storm cellar, my lambs! Run!'

The young 'uns' dog, Zip, began to yip. We streaked it to the house, where my dear wife Melissa was taking a rhubarb pie out of the oven.

'Twister coming, Mama!' Polly cried out.

'And heading this way!' Will added, glancing out the window.

We all tumbled down into the storm cellar and shut the slanting doors after us. We could hear a whistling in the air as that twister drew closer. There was nothing to do now but wait it out in the darkness underground.

'Do you think it'll carry off the house?' Jill asked.

'And your Franklin automobile, Pa?' asked Chester.

'Why, our farm's too trifling small for a whirlwind to go out of its way for,' I said. 'Nothing to worry about, my lambs.'

But the whistling in the air became a screech and we knew that cyclone wasn't far off. The screech became a howl and we knew it was closer still. The howl became a roar and we knew that infernal twister was upon us!

The young 'uns covered their ears. Mercy! The very earth shook. Overhead, we could hear the house windows explode. And for a last moment it seemed that all the air in the cellar was sucked up and away. At least, I believe that's what made our hair shoot up on end.

Then the roar faded to a howl, and the howl to a screech, and the screech to a whistle. I was dead certain our house had gone up in sticks and the air-cooled Franklin automobile with it. I scampered up into the daylight.

'Glory be!' I shouted. 'Come see for yourselves!'

The house was still standing. And the Franklin, too!

But our joy hardly lasted a moment. That infernal freak of nature had come so close it had plucked our entire crop of ripe red tomatoes, vines, stakes and all.

Worse than that – *it had sucked up our powerful rich topsoil*. Every glorious handful! We found ourselves gazing at a one-acre hole in the ground where our farm had been. You'd think that tricksy twister had paused a moment to scoop it out clean.

'Oh, Pa.' My dear wife Melissa began to cry, and the girls joined in.

I set my jaws and strode towards the old Franklin. 'Dry your tears, my loves,' I said. 'That whirlwind is bound to tucker itself out and drop our farm somewhere. I aim to race after it.'

Well, the Franklin was still standing, but in no condition to race. Tarnation! that pesky tornado had sucked the air out of the tyres.

'Will – fetch the tyre pump,' I said. 'Not a moment to lose!'

The boys and I took turns pumping up the tyres. We had hardly got started when Zip sniffed out something

alive cowering under the car. Peter crawled underneath and dragged the creature out.

No. It wasn't the Great Prairie Hidebehind.

But it was a mighty odd beast – never saw anything like it before. It appeared to be a small mountain goat with the tail and ears of a large white-tailed jack rabbit – but that wasn't what made it odd. No, indeed, the surprising thing was its legs. The beast wasn't constructed to stand on level ground. The legs on one side were amazing short and the legs on the other were amazing long. The poor creature

was a bit dazed – it must have fallen out of the tornado along the way.

We had got the last tyre pumped up when the girls gave a shout. Polly had run into the house to find the natural history book and turned up a picture of that wrong-legged beast. 'Pa, it's a Sidehill Gouger!' she said.

Oh, it was mighty rare, the book said. It lived on steep hillsides and needed those two long legs and two short legs to walk upright. Of course, it went round and round one way only – it would tumble over if it tried to go the other.

'Can we keep it, Pa?' the girls asked, one after the other.

'We don't have any steep hillsides around here,' I re-minded them, and jumped into the Franklin. Will and Chester jumped in, too. They wanted to go chasing after that cyclone with me.

Well, it wasn't hard to follow. Gracious, no! It had not only snatched up our tomatoes, but emptied a bin of onions and sucked up three barrels of cider vinegar I had set out to age. You could see that twister for miles, spinning away as red as ketchup.

In fact, it *was* ketchup. As we raced along we could see it squirting everything in its path – barns, windmills and a bald-headed fellow tacking up KEEP OUT signs who hadn't dodged out of the way fast enough. He said later it was the best tomato ketchup he had ever tasted, though it was a mite gritty. But he didn't mind that. Our topsoil in that ketchup tornado had grown hair on his head.

Well, we must have chased that whirlwind forty miles

across the prairie. About the last thing it found to rip up was a stretch of barbed-wire. Then it ran out of mischief, so to speak. It dropped our farm in a great red heap and wasted away to the small end of nothing.

When we reached our pile of topsoil we could hardly believe our eyes. That freak of nature had not only fenced it with tomato stakes and barbed-wire – it had even tacked up the KEEP OUT signs.

'Pa, how'll we ever fetch it home?' Chester asked.

I scratched my head. It looked like two hundred wagon-loads, at least, sitting on someone else's land. We'd be lucky if they didn't charge storage. My, what a heap of money it would cost to haul that farm forty miles back where it came from!

'Boys,' I said softly. 'Might as well head back home. Looks like we're tornadoed out of business. Unless we can figure some way to raise a mighty sum of money.'

Just then Will pricked up his ears. 'Hear that, Pa? Sounds like a tin tea-kettle steaming away.'

'There are no tea-kettles out here,' I said.

'I hear it too,' Chester said. 'And *there* it is!'

Well, it wasn't a tin tea-kettle. It was a peculiar-looking bird wailing away inside the barbed-wire fence. *Mighty* peculiar. For one thing, it wore its feet backwards.

No. It wasn't the Great Hairy Prairie Hidebehind.

The boys crawled through the barbed-wire and fetched the sad creature. It was about the size of a small turkey, only larger, and the cyclone had plucked all its feathers. The most surprising feature was its beak. It was shaped like the spout of a tea-kettle, and every time the bird made that tea-kettle-boiling sound – why, steam came pouring out.

I shook my head in amazement. 'I declare if that twister

hasn't flushed some mighty uncommon livestock out of hiding,' I said.

'Can we take it home?' the boys asked.

I shook my head, and cranked the Franklin. 'With all its feathers gone the poor thing's bound to expire.'

Well, the boys packed that nameless bird in ketchupy topsoil mud and before we had driven three miles a new crop of feathers began to sprout! They were the colour of green tea, except the tail feathers. Those were sterling silver and shaped like teaspoons.

All the way back we saw dazed chickens and pigs and prairie dogs caught up by that howling twister and spun away far from home. But the boys had lost interest in common barnyard animals. They now fancied themselves rare game collectors.

We couldn't have been more than a mile from home when Will shouted, 'There's something, Pa!'

The boys jumped out and started chasing a catfish through the dust.

Well, there's nothing uncommon about a catfish — but this one appeared to be swimming through the dust *backwards*. Making good time, too. Gave the boys a merry chase!

They did manage to corral the confused fish. They flopped him in the back seat, and we rushed on home to get him in a tub of water before it was too late. I reckoned the twister had whirlwinded him out of a creek somewhere.

But I was dead wrong. That ungrateful rascal leaped right out of the water back into the dust. It had a considerable *dislike* for water.

Turned out the boys had caught a genuine Desert Vamooser — very rare. It swims tail-first to keep the dust out of its eyes.

And wasn't I surprised to see how that wrong-legged Sidehill Gouger had made himself right at home! There he was running around the sides of our one-acre hole in the ground, anti-clockwise, happy as a squirrel, and pausing only to gouge out shallow and mysterious pockets.

The young 'uns turned the Desert Vamooser loose in the bottom and I gathered the family together to break the bad news about our topsoil.

'Maybe another twister will come along and fetch it back,' Polly said hopefully.

That wasn't likely, and Mama began dabbing at her eyes with her apron. 'I must have left the tea-kettle boiling,' she remarked suddenly.

Mercy! We had forgot that shy, spout-nosed, vapour-blowing creature in the back of the car, and it had got lonely. The young 'uns crowded around and gazed at it in wonder.

'Look, Pa, its feet point behind it,' Larry said.

Well, it didn't take long to discover what nature of bird the boys had found. It was a Silver-Tailed Tea-kettler – very rare. The book said no hunter had ever tracked one down to pluck its wonderful sterling silver tail feathers.

And little wonder! I reckoned we knew something that wasn't in the book – those wrong-way feet. We let it out and saw that it left backward footprints. My, that was clever! Anyone following those tracks would proceed where the Tea-kettler had *been*, not where it was *going*.

'Pa,' Little Clarinda blurted out. 'We've got us a zoo. Our very own zoo! We could charge a penny.'

'A nickel,' Larry declared.

'A dime,' Mary said.

'A quarter, at least,' Tim insisted. 'Didn't Pa say it will take a heap of cash money to fetch back the farm?'

A zoo! The thought near took my breath away. Wouldn't folks come from miles around to see these rare creatures? It wouldn't surprise me if we had the only Tea-kettler, Desert Vamooser and Sidehill Gouger in captivity.

'Glory be!' I exclaimed. 'A zoo, did you say? Why, a zoo we'll have! No telling what other rare beasts that twister twisted up and scattered along the way. Not a moment to lose, my lambs!'

Well, the young 'uns scurried after butterfly-nets and gunny sacks to go collecting – all except Will. 'Pa,' he called, stooping at the rear of the Franklin. 'Look at these tracks – coming all the way down the road. Far as the eye can see. I do believe something followed us home.'

My, but they were outlandish paw prints! Clearly a two-legged beast that appeared to walk only on the tips of its toes. Toes? Why it had *seventeen* toes – eight on the left foot, nine on the right.

'We must have scared it off,' I remarked, looking all about. And when the young 'uns turned up ready to set out, I said, 'Keep your eyes peeled for a seventeen-toed critter. That would be a fine catch for our zoo.'

Well, the whole family spread out along the twisty path of the tornado. By early candlelight we returned home with several uncommon beasts and birds, including a rare Spotted Compass Cat – its tail always pointed north. But we'd seen neither hide nor hair of that two-legged, seventeen-toed visitor.

What we did see – standing at the very edge of our one-acre hole in the ground – was a two-legged, hairy-faced varmint that I recognized to be a man. He had a shotgun in one hand, a deer rifle in the other, a revolver in his belt and a large skinning knife between his teeth.

He was raising the rifle to his shoulder when I gave a shout. 'What in tarnation do you think you're doing, sir! Who are you?'

The rifle exploded. 'Tarnation yourself!' he shouted. That man could talk with a skinning knife between his teeth. 'You made me miss! I wanted that Sidehill Gouger and mean to have him – stuffed and mounted. I'm a hunting man, that's who I am, and I've got a hunting licence to prove it.'

I was bristling mad. 'Well, you're trespassing and you don't have a licence for that. Furthermore and whatsmore, this is a zoo, sir, and you can't hunt in a zoo.'

'A *zoo*!' he laughed. That man could even laugh with the skinning knife between his teeth. 'I don't see any signs. Light's failing. I'll be back.'

Of course, I stood guard all night long. The young'uns busied themselves making signs and we posted them all around our farm.

McBROOM'S ZOO
No Hunting Allowed!

Well, that fellow didn't show up at the crack of dawn. But a flock of sage hens did. They made nests in the hillside gouges the Sidehill Gouger had gouged out. I declare – those hens had been searching for him!

It turned out they weren't true sage hens. They were

118

Galoopus Birds – very rare. Nesting in the steepest places, the Galoopus laid square eggs so they couldn't roll off down the slopes.

As the morning brightened I noticed there were more of those tiptoe tracks about – and very fresh.

'Jill,' I said. 'Is there anything in the natural history book about a seventeen-toed animal?'

She went to look it up while the other young 'uns scampered off to post signs announcing the opening of our zoo. That flock of Galoopus Birds would be a fine addition, not to mention the critters we had brought back in gunny sacks the day before. The prize of the lot was a toothy, moose-headed Spitback Giascutus, and it did come in handy.

For just then that two-legged, hairy-faced hunting man turned up. I did wonder if he had seventeen toes, but he was wearing boots.

'You can see the signs,' I snapped.

'Oh, I can see the signs,' he chuckled between the skinning knife in his teeth. 'But I can't read.'

Quick as lightning he raised the rifle and fired. I thought sure he had bagged our Sidehill Gouger, but no, he had taken a sudden fancy to the moose-headed Giascutus. And that was a mistake. No one had *ever* been able to shoot a Spitback Giascutus.

What happened next was truly amazing! The Giascutus raised its antlers and caught the lead ball between its teeth. He spit it right back with remarkable aim and took a nick out of that infernal hunter's left ear.

Didn't he leave in a hurry, though! He'd never been shot at by an animal before. But I feared he'd be back.

Jill came hurrying out of the house with the book. 'Pa, the only seventeen-toed creature known is the Great

Seventeen-Toed Hairy Prairie Hidebehind – and it's extinct.'

'Extinct?' I replied, thoughtfully. 'Well, it may be extinct in the book, but there's one alive and lurking around here somewhere. And I declare if those don't look like fresh tracks just behind you.'

I didn't mean to scare her – but she did jump back. Not that there was a creature to be seen. According to the book no one had *ever* laid eyes on a Hidebehind. It was always hiding behind something. Oh, it was slick at the game. A Hidebehind could be following you on its tiptoes, but it did no good to look. Every time you spun around it would still be hiding behind you!

Well, the news spread quickly that we had a dry-land fish that swam backwards and birds that laid square eggs. A few folks turned up, and then more folks, and before long whole crowds of folks – some from the next state! The young 'uns charged a quarter – kids free – and took turns lecturing on the surprising habits of our animals.

My, didn't we do a brisk business! Mama made barrels of lemonade and I slept in the daytime so I could stand watch at night. That hunter with all his guns was a worry.

And I did mean to have a look at the Great Seventeen-Toed Hairy Prairie Hidebehind.

I tell you, it was a mite scary guarding the zoo at night. I was certain that Hidebehind was following me about, but every time I whirled around it whirled around too. I even tried walking with a hand mirror, but the Hidebehind was too eternal clever for tricks like that.

But one night when I whirled around I saw that pesky hunter sneaking down among the zoo animals. He barely got his rifle raised before the Tea-kettler steamed out a warning. The Desert Vamooser streaked backwards and threw a large fishtail full of dust into his eyes. Ruined his aim, of course – near blinded him for a month, it seemed.

By that time we had raised enough cash money to cart back our topsoil. Everyone agreed we had best turn the uncommon creatures back into the wild where they belonged. Of course, the young 'uns hated to part with them. And I do believe the animals were happy with us. But there was the danger they would end up, one by one, on that two-legged varmint's wall – stuffed and mounted.

So the next morning we took down the zoo signs and loaded up the car with animals – mercy, there was hardly room for the young 'uns! – and took off for the wildest parts of the prairie. We found a dusty old river-bed for the Desert Vamooser, but it fell dark before we discovered a sidehill for the Sidehill Gouger. We didn't rightly know what sort of country the Silver-Tailed Tea-kettler came from, but it began to steam happily as we ran through a patch of poison ivy and we dropped it off there.

Well, you might think we'd get lost chasing about in the middle of the night in the middle of nowhere – far from it. Didn't we have that Compass Cat with its tail always pointing due north? It was the last animal we turned loose.

Our farm? Oh, we got the topsoil hauled back – the wagons stretched out for half a mile and it took the better part of a week. But my thoughts were still on that Great Seventeen-Toed Hairy Prairie Hidebehind. Every morning I found fresh tracks. I *did* want to have a look at it. I began practising whirling about – faster and faster.

Well, I got mighty fast. Before breakfast one morning I was out by the well and felt certain I was being followed. I whirled about quick as you please – and saw that backward-footed Silver-Tailed Tea-kettler. It had come back.

'Will*jill*hester*chester*peter*polly*tim*tom*mary*larry*and-little*clarinda*!' I called, and they came bounding outside. 'Looks like that fellow means to stay. You've got a new pet.'

Well, they took the Tea-kettler inside the house – and just in time. Not a moment later that hairy-faced hunting man turned up armed to the teeth, as usual, and wearing goggles. He didn't mean to have dust thrown in his eyes again.

'You're too late,' I said. 'The animals are gone – every one.'

'I see fresh tracks,' he answered gleefully, lowering his nose to the ground like a bloodhound. 'Reckon I'll follow them and bag myself that big bird.'

He couldn't see too well with those goggles on. He overlooked the Hidebehind's paw prints and went loping away – following the Tea-kettler's backward tracks. As far as I know he followed them right back where they started – a hundred miles across the prairie in a patch of poison ivy. We never saw him again.

But I did see the Great Seventeen-Toed Hairy Prairie Hidebehind! Indeed, I did! Not that I ever learned to whirl about fast enough – without help.

It was dusk and I sat down on a small wood stump to shake a rock out of my shoe – only it wasn't a small wood stump. It was a porcupine with its quills up. Didn't I jump! And didn't I whirl about *quick*!

Glory be! There he stood – the Great Seventeen-Toed Hairy Prairie Hidebehind!

Well, that shy beast was so embarrassed to be seen that he immediately hid behind *himself*. At least, I reckon that's what happened, for he just seemed to spin out of sight. A few tufts of orange hair settled to the earth like feathers.

We never saw his tracks around our wonderful one-acre farm again. But I'm certain he's still lurking about somewhere, hiding behind someone. Of course, he's quite harmless.

Mercy! He could be hiding behind YOU.

THE PIEMAKERS

Helen Cresswell

Sometimes Gravella Roller felt she would scream if she
ever saw another pie, but it couldn't be helped. The fact
was that piemaking was in her blood. Her family, the
Danby Rollers, were piemakers through and through, and
nothing would change that now – why, even her name
Gravella was just 'Gravy' prettied up!

And the pies they made! Superb they were, with their
decorated crusts, succulent meat and luscious gravy. And
were they always good, those pies? Without fail? Yes, they
really were, until the great calamity of the pie that was
meant for a King but wasn't fit even for a pig, for didn't
the bakehouse break down only that night?

THE OGRE DOWNSTAIRS

Diana Wynne Jones

'Caspar and Johnny pelted up to Gwinny's room
regardless of noise. Johnny thought she was on fire, Caspar
thought that she was being eaten away by acids. They
burst into the room and stood staring. Gwinny did not
seem to be there. Her lamp was lit, her bed empty, her
window shut, and her dollshouse and other things
arranged around as usual, but they could not see Gwinny.

'She's gone,' said Caspar helplessly.

'No, I haven't,' said Gwinny, her voice quivering rather.
'I'm up here.' She appeared to be hanging from the
ceiling and looked a bit like a puppet. 'And I can't come
down,' she added.

She couldn't either. At least not until the *vol.pulv.*
splashed on her from Johnny's chemistry set had worn
off ...

DANNY THE CHAMPION OF THE WORLD

Roald Dahl

Danny's playroom was the workshop of his father's filling station. His first toys were the greasy cogs and springs and pistons that filled it. By the time he was seven he could take a small engine to pieces and put it together again – pistons and crankshaft and all. So being eight was a lot of fun.

As it turned out, the year he was nine was even more exciting, for Danny's father had a deep, dark secret, a secret he had kept hidden all Danny's life up till then, and soon after he'd revealed it Danny found himself engaged on a wild and difficult scheme. A wildly funny, wickedly inventive romp of a book, suitable for every age.

SUPER GRAN IS MAGIC

Forrest Wilson

Super Gran wasn't all that bothered about Mr Black's new invention: a small black box that could hypnotize people and animals. But then a rotten stage magician called Mystico thought of the perfect way to make his act more exciting: he'd set a hypnotized Super Gran to work for him. So suddenly Super Gran had to call on all her Super-powers! The fourth book about everyone's favourite senior citizen.

Heard about the Puffin Club?

... it's a way of finding out more about Puffin books and authors, of winning prizes (in competitions), sharing jokes, a secret code, and perhaps seeing your name in print! When you join you get a copy of our magazine, *Puffin Post*, sent to you four times a year, a badge and a membership book.

For details of subscription and an application form, send a stamped addressed envelope to:

The Puffin Club Dept A
Penguin Books Limited
Bath Road
Harmondsworth
Middlesex UB7 ODA

and if you live in Australia, please write to:

The Australian Puffin Club
Penguin Books Australia Limited
P.O. Box 257
Ringwood
Victoria 3134